Do you smell smoke?

In the office building at the refinery, the red-orange flame that had been born as a tiny flicker had swelled and stretched into a thick, blazing vine of fire. Its greedy tendrils cleverly snaked their way from the basement to the first floor and upward via the wiring hidden between the walls.

On the second floor, a clerk sniffed the air. She swiveled in her chair to turn to a coworker and ask, "Do you smell smoke?"

MED CENTER

Virus

Flood

Fire

Blast

MED CENTER

DIANE HOH

SCHOLASTIC INC.
New York Toronto London Auckland Sydney

ISBN 0-590-67316-5

12 11 10 9 8 7 6 5 4 3 2   6 7 8 9/9 0 1/0

Printed in the U.S.A.   01

First Scholastic printing, September 1996

MED CENTER

fire

prologue

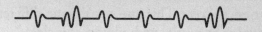

On the grounds of Grant Petroleum Products, a sprawling complex of oil tanks, office buildings, and warehouses, the darkness and quiet of a basement closet was broken by a sudden sharp, spitting sound, followed by a duller, hissing noise. Then a shower of golden, fiery sparks, like a cluster of fireflies, shot out of a large black electrical box fastened on one wall.

When the sparks and the hissing had died, there was silence again in the dim enclosure.

But minutes later, a tiny puff of smoke curled out from under the edges of the big black box on the wall. The box serviced one of several office buildings on the site, which spread across thickly wooded acreage in the city of Grant, Massachusetts. The office building, tall and wide and constructed entirely of red brick, had been built close to one of the huge, round oil tanks.

"Shouldn't be puttin' a building this close to the tanks," one of the construction workers had been heard to mutter while working on the site years earlier. "If old Titus Grant wasn't so tight with money, they'd be spreadin' this place out a little more, keepin' all the buildings away from the tanks. Me, I been around refineries all my life. Ain't seen one yet that didn't have a fire at least once a year. This one won't be no different. Shouldn't be puttin' no buildings this close."

But no one paid the slightest bit of attention to his objections. Although the refinery complex had grown over the years, the office building had stayed where it was, side by side with the cluster of oil tanks.

Now, the tiny puff of smoke grew. At first, it stayed close to the black box, trailing around its outside edges like a curling, gray vine. Then, fueled by oxygen in the air, it blossomed. Eager to explore its surroundings, it left the black box and began lazily easing its way up the basement wall toward the ceiling. As it did so, a small, bright orange-red flame stabbed its way out of the box, looked to see where the puff of smoke had gone, and decided to follow it.

The smoke and its tagalong partner, the flame, seemed to be in no particular hurry. They took their time easing along the wall, like children exploring new territory.

But as they went, they grew in size.

Miles away, in the center of the city, in another sprawling complex of taller, newer brick buildings known as Med Center, the staff settled in for a Saturday spent meeting every kind of medical emergency and rendering every kind of medical care. They were blissfully unaware of the refinery's lazy, trailing smoke and its companion, the flame. So they had no way of knowing what horrors were in store for them on this unusually balmy, windy Saturday in late October.

chapter
1

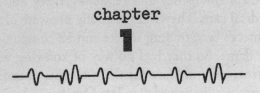

The sleek white limousine pulled up at Med Center's Emergency Services entrance and came to a halt.

"Hey, get a load of that!" Will Jackson said, nudging Susannah Grant with his elbow. Both worked in the Emergency Services at the huge medical complex, Will as a paramedic, Susannah as a volunteer. During a rare lull in what had been a hectic Saturday morning, they had been asked to straighten one of the waiting rooms. Although both thrived on the excitement of emergency care, that morning it was a relief to escape the steady parade of heart attacks, broken bones, sprained ankles, abdominal pain, allergic reactions, or asthma attacks.

Susannah, wearing jeans and her pink volunteer's smock, her long, wavy, blonde hair neatly ponytailed, had just finished rearranging a thick pile of magazines on a low, white plastic table beside the coffee machine when Will's elbow collided with hers.

She glanced up, deep blue eyes following Will's dark ones to the large expanse of glass overlooking Med Center's grounds, including the rear driveway. She saw the limousine, but took no notice of it. Her gaze traveled beyond it, still seeking whatever it was that had caught Will's attention. "What?" she finally asked.

"The car! The *car*." Then he added, sounding piqued, "Oh, I forgot. Limousines probably pull up into your driveway all the time. I guess the sight of one wouldn't mean a thing to you." He drew his tall, lanky body, in jeans and his navy blue paramedic's windbreaker, up to its full height and said archly, "But we don't see many of them over in Eastridge."

Susannah's cheeks reddened. Every time she thought that Will was getting over the fact that she was Susannah *Grant*, whose ancestors had founded the city of Grant and whose family lived in a house that had a name . . . okay, a *mansion* that had a name — Linden Hall — and sat all by itself high up on a hill overlooking the entire city, something like this happened to prove that it still bothered him. And she was reminded again that they lived in completely different worlds. His was Eastridge, Grant's mostly African-American community. Hers was the affluent West Side.

Every time something like this happened, the

few close moments they'd shared since they'd begun to work together in Emergency shrank in the face of their differences.

Like she cared where he lived. If Will was purple and lived in a tree house it wouldn't have made a difference to her. It wasn't just that he was so great-looking, his face strong-boned, his eyes warm, his smile slightly crooked, as if he wasn't sure he wanted to let it loose. He was kind and funny and smart, and a lot wiser about the world than any of the boys at her private day school. But he was also stiff-necked with pride, and very stubborn.

Which was what he was being right now. Could she help it if the sight of a limousine didn't impress her? He wasn't being fair. True, she had been seeing them at home all of her life. Many of her father's associates and friends used limousine services. But she'd also seen plenty of limos here at Med Center. The medical complex, its beautiful brick buildings scattered across acres of well-landscaped, rolling lawns, was world-famous. People came from all over to be treated at Emsee for one illness or another. Many of those people were rich. They sometimes arrived in limos. Will just didn't see them because he was usually out on an ambulance run.

"I wonder who's in it?" she queried aloud. It could be royalty. It wouldn't be the first time a prince or princess, maybe a count, had sought treatment at Med Center. Or it could be a famous lawyer, actor, artist, or banker. Emsee got all kinds of people. "Maybe that diplomat's nephew who was here last week, the one with the migraine? He seemed okay when he left, but he could have had another attack."

Susannah was one of only two teenagers who, after being carefully tested and interviewed, then attending a variety of classes, were allowed into treatment and trauma rooms at Grant Memorial Hospital. Grant was the largest of the hospitals at Med Center, and the only one with a fully staffed, fully equipped Emergency Department. Susannah had been on duty when a nephew of a diplomat was brought in. She had recognized the signs of migraine immediately, because her mother sometimes suffered from the agonizingly painful headaches. And she had held the patient's hand while Dr. Jonah Izbecki, her favorite physician at Emsee, examined him. Her heart had ached for the fourteen-year-old boy.

But the person who stepped confidently out of the limo when the uniformed chauffeur held the door open was not the diplomat's nephew. He had been tall and heavyset. Though shrouded in layers of dark, heavy clothing, the limo occupant was short and, judging by the size of the hands gloved in black leather and the black leather boot-clad foot that stepped out of the car, very slender. That was *all* Susannah could guess, because the eyes were invisible behind aviator sunglasses, and there was a wide-brimmed, brown suede hat pulled down over the hair and forehead.

Now *there* is someone who is trying to *hide*, Susannah thought with certainty. I wonder why?

She was just as certain, in spite of what was clearly a disguise, that the passenger leaving the limo was female. Anyone, she told herself, can put on dark pants, a cape, and a hat to hide who they are. But the way that person moves is absolutely feminine.

Two people — one a short, balding man in a gray business suit, the other a tall, wide-shouldered woman in a luxurious, full-length suede coat — emerged from the car. Both looked harried and unhappy. Each took a place on one side of the figure in sunglasses and, hands on her elbows, began hurrying her up the walkway.

Susannah grinned at Will. "I'm dying to know who that is. Beat you to the door," she challenged and, without waiting for his response, hurried out of the room.

Kate Thompson, the other student volunteer, was standing directly opposite Emergency's admissions desk when Susannah arrived. The two girls were the same height, but Kate carried herself with more authority, her head always high, her shoulders back, so she seemed taller. A beautiful girl with smooth skin the same chestnut shade as Will's, dark hair curving gently around high cheekbones, she leaned against the wall, an amused smile lighting beautiful doelike dark eyes. Her arms were folded against her version of the volunteer smock, a short, vividly printed dashiki in tones of rust, royal blue, and yellow. She put a finger to her lips as Susannah and Will reached her side. "Shh!" she cautioned. "You have to hear this. Wish I had a tape recorder on me. No one I know is going to believe it."

Susannah and Will obeyed, their eyes on the trio at the desk as they listened.

" . . . And of course I'll need several hours of privacy every day for my manicurist and my hairstylist and for Tina, who is an absolute wizard when it comes to skin," a young, assured voice was saying to the nurse behind the desk. The nurse was Kate's mother, Emergency's head nurse, Astrid Thompson. "That means," the new patient continued, "that while my *people* are here, there must be no nurses coming in to take my temperature or blood or any of those gross things. Antoine, that's my hairdresser, simply won't tolerate being interrupted. And then," the voice went on without pause, "I'll need a room for Bess here, my agent, and Jules, my manager. I'd like the rooms to be connecting, please, and they *must*, of course, have their own private baths."

Will muttered, "She must have us confused

with a four-star hotel." He grinned. "Wait till she tries to call room service."

The two adults protested that they had no intention of moving into the hospital. "We'll be here as much as you need us, Amber," the agent said, "but the staff here will take very good care of you."

The incoming patient seemed surprised, then angry, to learn that her agent and manager would not be at her side twenty-four hours a day. She was very vocal about this change in her plans.

"Who *is* she?" Susannah asked.

Kate and Will shook their heads. "Beats me," Kate said. "But even if she's *not* someone important, she sure *thinks* she is."

"This is not a hotel," Astrid Thompson told the new arrival in a brisk, no-nonsense voice. "But we will certainly do everything in our power to make you comfortable, Miss Taylor."

"Oh, please," the tall woman in suede said quickly, her voice hushed but clear to the three eavesdropping, "the doctor assured us that Amber would be registered under her real name, Emma Slocum. He made arrangements for her to check in here instead of in the main lobby, where she might be seen. The press, you know . . ."

Astrid Thompson nodded. "Yes, of course, I see the notation here. My mistake. Sorry."

Kate, Susannah, and Will exchanged puzzled glances. The press? So this Amber Taylor *was* someone important.

"Never heard of her," Kate said. "Have you?"

"Nope," Will answered quickly, and Susannah shook her head no.

But it was clear to all three of them that whoever Amber Taylor was, she expected first-class treatment at Emsee.

"I'll need a television set and a VCR," the girl went on. The cap and sunglasses remained in place. "And from one to two o'clock every afternoon, absolutely *no* one is to be allowed in my room, that's a must."

"I'm not sure that will be possible," the head nurse said smoothly. "We have our own schedule, Miss Tay . . . Miss Slocum, and we have many, many patients. We cannot possibly rearrange everyone else's routine to meet the needs of one person. I'm sure you understand."

"From one to two," she replied emphatically. "Absolutely no one in my room. That's final."

"I'm sure they'll do the best they can, Amber," the tall woman said hastily. "Jules, take her on up to her suite, before some eagle-eyed local reporter spots her. I'll handle the paperwork here."

As the man led her away, Amber called over her shoulder, "And I do not *ever* eat dead cows. If I see so much as one shred of disgusting beef on a dinner tray, heads will roll!"

"Sorry," the woman in suede apologized to Nurse Thompson when the girl and her manager had disappeared inside an elevator. "I'd love to excuse her behavior by saying she's very frightened about this illness, which no one has been able to diagnose. Actually, I think she probably *is* frightened. But it's also true that this is pretty much how she behaves even when she's *not* frightened. The girl has had too much fame, too fast. She's only seventeen. That is far too young to handle so much attention." The woman sighed and focused her attention on the papers Astrid had slid across the desk toward her. "Ah, well, that's youth. Were we ever that young and pampered?"

Kate's mother laughed wryly. "That young, sure. But never that pampered."

When the agent had completed the necessary paperwork, she went upstairs to check on the patient.

Kate, Susannah, and Will were nearly bursting with curiosity. Too much fame, too fast? The new patient was *their* age. Why didn't they know who she was?

"Let's follow her," Kate said impulsively. "I'm dying to see how she reacts to her johnny," referring to the plain white cotton hospital gown all patients at Emsee wore. "She probably arrived with a suitcase of pure silk gowns to wear. I wouldn't want to miss the fireworks when she finds out we've got a dress code that doesn't include silk." Her grin was almost wicked. She ran over to the desk to ask her mother if they could all take their break at the same time.

Astrid glanced around the unusually quiet corridor and waiting rooms. "Hard to believe, but I think we're actually seeing a few moments of peace and quiet. Might as well take your break while you can. I'm sure this lull won't last."

Kate's eyes were glistening with barely restrained glee as she ran back to Will and Susannah. "Miss Fame and Fortune is probably headed for the VIP suite on the fourth floor. Let's go watch her reaction to our accommodations," she said, and led the way to the elevator.

They were stopped in their tracks by the dying wails of not one, but two ambulances arriving at the same time.

Nurse Thompson called out to them, "Hold the phone! Don't take another step! I may need you."

Reluctantly, all three turned and hurried to the rear entrance. "I'll bet it's Handymen," Susannah said as they held the double glass doors open for the paramedics. "This is Saturday, remember."

Handymen was what Astrid Thompson called both men *and* women who reserved the weekend for experimentation with fancy new power tools. Saturday was the day home owners spent attempting to build decks, fences, and wooden playscapes for their children. In the process, they often came close to losing a limb, a finger, sometimes even a life. They came to Emsee to be sewn back together.

Susannah was right. The first ambulance contained a forty-three-year-old male with a bloody gash on his left arm, the result of his first encounter with a power saw. The injured forearm was wrapped in a blood-soaked towel. The man's face was chalk-white, and damp with perspiration. He's in shock, Susannah thought. She wasn't surprised. He had lost a lot of blood.

The second gurney carried a sculptor in her thirties wearing denim coveralls and safety glasses. The glasses had protected her eyes from the flame of the blowtorch she'd impulsively used to destroy a nest of bees in the wall of her garage. But she had neglected to wear gloves. Her left hand was burned badly. She, too, was in shock, and lay on the gurney silent and unmoving.

Susannah and Will ran with the power-saw injury into the suture room, while Kate and Astrid went with the burn patient to a treatment cubicle.

chapter
2

—∿∿∿—

"**M**an," Will whispered to Susannah as they arrived in the suture room and Dr. Jonah Izbecki took over, "the guy did a job on himself!"

When an IV had been established to stabilize the man's blood pressure and the wound had been examined, the doctor asked brusquely for "some eight gloves, one percent Xylocaine plain, and five-O prolene. Medium needle."

Susannah glanced nervously around the room. Nurse Thompson was in another room helping with the burn patient. And the short, blonde Nurse Carter, who was supposed to be in the room, was absent, too. Will was a paramedic who spent most of his time in the ambulance and knew very little about where hospital supplies were kept. That left only *her* to gather the necessary supplies for Izbecki. *Her!*

Except for the gloves, which she often brought to doctors who were about to suture, she had no idea where the other things were kept. Volunteers didn't fetch those things, the nurses did. Thanks to her classes, she knew *what* they all were. She just didn't know *where* they were. Why didn't anyone *tell* her these things?

Most of the staff was wary of her, afraid that if they made a mistake, she'd run home to Samuel Grant II and report their carelessness. The people who knew her well, like Kate, Astrid, and Will, knew she would never do that. But the rest of the staff tended to steer clear of Samuel Grant's daughter. Now, when she needed to know where certain things were kept, she didn't have a clue.

It was all so ridiculous. Her father didn't even *run* the hospital. Samuel Grant II kept himself busy with the oil refinery and Grant Pharmaceuticals, the massive lab located at the edge of Med Center's grounds. The enormous job of running the medical complex itself belonged to Caleb Matthews, father of nasty Callie Matthews, which was why Callie strutted around Emsee as if she owned the place.

Still, Samuel Grant II *was* on Med Center's board of directors, and everyone knew he paid attention to what went on in the complex. Susannah couldn't really blame the staff for being cautious around his daughter. But if they'd just tell her where things *were* . . .

"The prolene?" Dr. Izbecki asked impatiently.

Susannah was spared the humiliating experience of admitting she didn't know where to look for it by the sudden appearance of Nurse Carter.

"Sorry," she murmured, hurrying over to yank open drawers for the necessary supplies. She handed Susannah a fresh roll of gauze. Susannah was grateful to be included. "I heard the refinery siren," the nurse said as she filled the suture tray. "My husband's working over there this weekend, so I had to make a quick call to see what was going on."

The doctor reached for the gloves. "And?"

"False alarm, I guess. I talked to the operator. She said she hadn't heard anything about a fire." The nurse took up a position beside the gurney, the suture tray in her hands. "That siren gives me the creeps. Every time I hear it, my heart jumps into my throat. Tommy says the refinery pays too well to quit. Personally, I'd rather be poor and have some peace of mind than be worried about him all the time."

Dr. Izbecki began to stitch, carefully and precisely but efficiently. The man, his wound numbed by the Xylocaine, made no sound, and color had begun to return to his beefy face. "Let's just hope they're right about it being a false alarm," the doctor commented, drawing the needle out and inserting it again. "The last thing we need is a fire."

When the doctor completed the procedure, the nurse said to Susannah, "You can go now, Grant. They might need you with that burn patient. It looked pretty bad to me."

Wishing she could have been more help, Susannah nodded, and left the room. Will went with her. But the woman with the injured hand had already been sedated and wheeled off through one of the enclosed passageways to the Walter E. Miller Burn Unit at Med Center.

When Susannah and Kate had finished preparing the room for the next patient, they all returned to the nurses' station. The waiting room was beginning to fill up again. "Spare me from do-it-yourselfers," Astrid said grimly. "Any money that woman saved going after those bees herself is pocket change compared to what it will take to make that hand work properly again. If it ever does."

Before Susannah went into the waiting room to help with medical forms, she asked, "Did anyone else hear the refinery fire siren? The nurse in the suture room said she did."

"Yeah, I did." Kate adjusted a heavy wooden earring she had made herself. "About fifteen minutes ago. But I think it was only one blast, although it's hard to hear from in here. If the fire is serious, the siren is supposed to sound three times."

Will nodded. "Besides, if there's even the possibility of trouble, we'd get a call to send ambulances out there, on standby. No one's called yet, as far as I know."

He had barely finished speaking when a different kind of call came in. "See the man at 805 Linden Hill Boulevard. Possible heart attack."

Will was off and running toward the ambulance garage.

"Where's he off to?" The boy who came around a corner just then was shorter than Will, and heavier. Jeremy Barlow's father was Thomas Barlow, Chief Cardiologist at Grant Memorial. Jeremy hung around the hospital often, hoping to spend some time with the only parent available to him since his mother had left for San Francisco to become a writer. Kate and Susannah were accustomed to seeing Jeremy's thick, blonde hair, light blue eyes, and square, solemn face appear around one corner or another.

"He's going on an ambulance run," Susannah answered. "Heart attack, probably." She thought how depressing it must be to have nothing more fun to do on a gorgeous Saturday than hang around the hospital. Why wasn't Jeremy out doing something fun with friends?

Because we're all *here*, came the answer. Except for Sam, her own twin brother and one of Jeremy's friends. And Abby O'Connor, Susannah's closest friend. But while Abby was Susannah's best friend, Abby and Jeremy were too different to be close friends. Jeremy simmered, Abby bubbled, it was that simple. They had very little in common. Still, Susannah was sure that if Abby knew Jeremy was wandering around alone on a

Saturday, she'd have included him in any plans she had. Abby was like that.

Clipboard in hand, Susannah moved to the waiting room to find out which patients had sprains, which had stomachaches, which had swallowed a foreign object.

When she returned to the desk, where Kate and Jeremy were talking, Kate said impishly, "You haven't forgotten our celebrity, have you?" She quickly filled Jeremy in on Emsee's newest arrival. "Come on, let's go up and check her out while the going is good! Mom and Nurse Carter can handle what's in the waiting room."

Jeremy and Susannah followed Kate to the elevator.

At Zooey's, a popular hangout not far from Med Center, Abby O'Connor sat at a table with Susannah's twin brother, Sam, and Sid Costello. Sid's wheelchair was parked beside the table. Abby had moved her own chair as close as possible, so she and Sid could hold hands. When she heard the single blast of the refinery whistle, her brows drew together in a frown. "Oh, no!" Round, dark eyes framed in thick lashes fastened on Sid. "You don't think there's a fire, do you? It's not the right time of the year. Refinery fires are almost always in the summer."

"Not always," Sid disagreed. A good-looking boy with shoulder-length brown wavy hair, his eyes as dark as Abby's, he sat up very straight in the wheelchair. Anyone seeing him in it for the first time might have thought he was just trying it out on a lark. But he wasn't. A fall from the top of a water tower had left Sid paralyzed from the waist down and ended his football career at Grant High. No one seemed to know yet whether or not the condition was permanent. "We've had refinery fires in the fall, too. If the trees are already bare, it's harder for the fire to jump from tree to tree, so it's not as dangerous in the fall. But," glancing out the restaurant's wide window, he added, "this fall's been warm, and hardly any of the trees have lost their leaves. What's worse, the leaves are dry as toast."

"Nothing like looking on the bright side," Sam said dryly. "Is that what they teach you at Rehab, Costello?"

Sid shrugged his massive shoulders. Under Rehab's steady regimen of physical therapy, his upper-body strength was increasing rapidly. Sam's remark didn't bother him. Sam Grant III never took anything seriously. Privately, Sid thought Sam would have learned to do just that after hosting that stupid party during the last flood and nearly drowning his own friends. Sam was just lucky they'd all survived. The episode hadn't seemed to change him at all. Maybe nothing ever would.

Abby was still tilting her head, listening, "I

only heard one blast," she said, playing nervously with her straw wrapper. "That's good, right? Just one. If it was a real fire, the siren wouldn't have stopped."

"Right." Sam finished his drink and stood, zipping up his red athletic jacket. He yanked a few crisp bills from a wallet and tossed the money onto the blue Formica table. "Like you said, it's not the right time of year for a refinery fire. Let's go cruise around and see what's happening in this thriving metropolis, okay? I'm tired of sitting."

Abby stood up, too, slipping into a brown suede bomber jacket. Sam dwarfed her. Abby often wished she were taller, like Susannah, but whenever that wish popped into her mind, she quickly told herself she wouldn't want to *be* Susannah, and that took care of it. She'd rather live in her own crazy household full of noise and younger siblings and chaos than in that house on the hill. Linden Hall was so enormous, it always seemed empty when she went there with Susannah. Like Sam, Susannah's parents were so busy socially, they were hardly ever home, and the household staff pretty much stayed out of sight. Nope, she'd rather be short and five pounds overweight and have to do the dishes every other night and make her own bed than be Susannah Grant, the girl who supposedly had everything.

Abby didn't normally hang out with Sam Grant, even though his sister was her closest friend. He was too much of a party person to suit her. But she hadn't pulled volunteer duty at Rehab on this warm, sunny Saturday, and had dropped into Zooey's for a Coke, looking for something interesting to do. To her delight, Sid was there. Sam had picked him up at Rehab and brought him to Zooey's, as he did occasionally. Thanks to Sam, and to Sid's other friends, who seemed to number in the hundreds, Sid was getting away from Rehab more often these days. He seemed a lot less self-conscious about the ever-present wheelchair. He'd taken to calling it his *chariot*. He'd changed a lot since she'd first met him during a volunteer shift at Rehab. Lost in self-pity, he'd been rude, patronizing, and demanding. Sometimes he still was when he became impatient with his progress.

"We could take a ride out to the refinery, just to make sure," Abby suggested. She needed to see with her own eyes that there was no fire.

"Oh, now *there's* a good time," Sam said sarcastically. "I can't imagine why I didn't have that penciled in on my calendar."

"Sa-am! Come on. My dad *works* there. And I'm not sure, but I think he said he had to go in to work today, even though it's Saturday. So please? It won't take that long." When Sam didn't answer, her voice took on a slightly acid tone. "Or you can drop me off at my house and go find some really *interesting* people."

Sam laughed and reached out to chuck her under the chin. "I didn't say you weren't interesting, O'Connor. Not that you've ever given me the chance to find out. I just said a trip to the refinery isn't my idea of a good time. But if you really want to go check things out, I'll drive. Let's go. Costello, you'll have to come, too, since I'm taxiing you around."

"I could wheel my way back to Rehab in my chariot here," Sid countered, patting the wheels on his chair. "But," flashing Abby the grin that she loved, "I'd rather stick with O'Connor. She looks worried. Can't have that, now, can we?"

Abby smiled at him, but said, "I'm not worried. I'm just . . . well, I just want to make sure everything's okay over there, that's all."

When they were outside, she sniffed the air for smoke. Frowning into the bright sunshine, the breeze warm on her face, she smelled nothing but autumn, heavy in the air. So she breathed a small sigh of relief, and relaxed as she climbed into Sam's shiny silver van. Sam lifted Sid in to sit beside her, then hoisted the folded wheelchair into the back.

In the office building at the refinery, the red-orange flame that had been born as a tiny flicker had swelled and stretched into a thick, blazing vine of fire. Its greedy tendrils cleverly snaked their way from the basement to the first floor and upward via the wiring hidden between the walls.

On the second floor, a clerk sniffed the air. She swiveled in her chair to turn to a coworker and ask, "Do you smell smoke?"

The woman, busy typing invoices, laughed and said, "Oh, *you*, Clara! You're always smelling smoke. I've worked beside you for nine years, and not a day has gone by that you haven't smelled smoke. You should *not* be working in a refinery. Get a job over at the boutique in town. We'll all be happier. The only thing I smell is the tuna-fish sandwich I brought for lunch."

On the third floor, a maintenance worker in a gray uniform, installing new pulls on a metal filing cabinet, lifted his head, glanced around him, sniffed the air as the clerk had, then shook his head and returned to his task.

Ten minutes later, the flames burst through a first-floor wall into an employee lounge in an explosion of heat, smoke, and fire. The six people inside the room had been lazily sipping hot coffee and discussing Grant High's football win of the night before.

Brendan O'Connor, father of Susannah Grant's best friend, Abby, had just finished saying, "Is it me or is it hot in here? Thermostat must be on the fritz!" when the wall blew.

Fire, heat, and smoke burst into the room. A section of flaming wallboard hit Abby's father on the back of his head, knocking him to the white asphalt tile floor.

Though the blow was severe, Brendan O'Connor was not too stunned to realize as he hit the tile that the floor was very, very hot. *Burning* hot.

Then he lost consciousness.

chapter
3

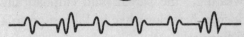

Kate, Jeremy, and Susannah weren't disappointed when they reached the VIP suite on the fourth floor and took up positions outside the door, which was slightly ajar. They were able to hear perfectly, and what they heard was exactly what Kate had anticipated.

"I can't wear *this*!" a young, feminine voice cried from inside. "It's *white*!"

Susannah, peering in through the opening, could see the bed, a suitcase opened on it, the figure shrouded in dark clothing, and a hand holding up one of Emsee's white cotton gowns. The hand was no longer gloved. It was small and delicate. "It'll make me look like I've already *died*! Bess, you know it will. I do not ever, *ever* wear white. Anyway, they forgot to put a zipper or buttons up the back. This thing doesn't even *close*. Forget it. I'm not wearing this."

"Everyone wears them, Amber," the woman answered. Her voice sounded tense and tired. "They're standard hospital gear."

Suzanne watched as the hand released the

27

gown and let it fall to the floor, where it lay in a heap. The same hand reached inside the open suitcase to pull out a short, red gown. Silk, Susannah decided. Just like Kate said. "*This* is what I'm wearing," the patient said emphatically. "If the doctors here don't like it, I'll just go to a different hospital."

"This is the hospital that can help you," the man's deep voice said. "You heard the doctor in New York. He swears by this place."

"*She's from New York City,*" Susannah whispered over her shoulder to Kate and Jeremy.

"He said," the man continued, "that this is the best place to find out why you're having those attacks. Why you have trouble breathing sometimes, and what's causing those awful headaches." His voice was sympathetic, cajoling. "You know how you hate those headaches. You can't work when you have them. We're here to take care of that, Amber."

"This room won't do at all," the girl's voice continued, as if her manager hadn't spoken. "I thought you said this was the VIP suite. There's no *fridge*. And that horrible flowery print on the furniture is sickening. The walls are peach, Jules. *Peach!* That's almost as bad as white. And where is my TV? I *have* to have a TV!"

The sympathetic voice hardened. "Look, kid, can we talk reality here? I can't believe Leo gave you this time off. You need to be in and out of here faster than you can say unemployment line, or Leo might just decide you're replaceable. This is your career we're talking about here. So let's not sweat the small stuff like Med Center's set design and wardrobe, okay? Let's just get you fixed up and back to New York before people start asking whatever happened to Amber Taylor."

Susannah moved a cautious step closer to the doorway in time to see the patient whirl. The sunglasses and hat had been removed, revealing stunning, deep blue eyes and a carefully tousled long dark mane of curls. The face was very pretty, almost beautiful, although there was a petulant look about the mouth, and the clear, smooth skin had gone alabaster-white with shock.

Behind Susannah, Jeremy breathed, "Oh, man, she's a knockout!"

"Replace me?" the girl cried, her tone a mixture of anxiety and anger. She turned to appeal to the woman. "That can't happen! It won't, will it, Bess? Leo would never replace me, would he? He couldn't!"

"No, no, of course not, dear. Don't think about it, okay?" The woman moved into Susannah's view as she shot the manager a look of reproof. "You're here to get well, and I don't want you thinking about anything else. Never fear, I'll handle Leo. I've dealt with far worse than Leo McCullough, believe me."

Outside, a siren split the air. Startled, the patient jumped nervously. "What was *that*?"

"Just an ambulance," the manager said. "You'll be hearing that sound a lot. This *is* a hospital."

"The building isn't soundproofed?" The girl sounded horrified. "Then you will have to get me earplugs," she added commandingly, moving out of Susannah's line of vision. "I can't sleep with *that* racket going on!"

Susannah whispered over her shoulder to Jeremy and Kate, *"That was no ambulance. That was the refinery siren. I wonder if there really is a fire."* She wasn't unduly alarmed. Refinery fires were common in Grant. There was at least one every year, sometimes more. Although there had been some very serious fires over the years, most of the time they were put out quickly, with little damage to property, and few severe injuries.

Still, that shrill, insistent sound never failed to rattle her.

"We'd better go back downstairs," Kate said. "See what's going on. If there *is* a fire, even a small one, we might be needed. Break time's over for us."

As they left, they could hear clearly the new patient's voice complaining about the hospital-issue slippers for her feet. "These are *too* stupid!

They have no heels at all. I'm too *short* without heels. I'm not wearing them, *ever*, so you might as well toss them right now."

Kate held the incredulous laughter in until they were safely inside the elevator. Then she let it out. "She expected high-heeled slippers?" she cried, gasping for breath. "Maybe a pair of red satin mules with ostrich feathers, like in the movies? Who does she think she *is*?" When her laughter had died, she asked, "So, who do you guys think she is? A princess, maybe? We had one here in July, remember? What a brat she was! This new one sounds just like her, except without the accent."

"Susannah said she's from New York," Jeremy reminded Kate. "I don't know that much about New York City, but I'm pretty sure it's not run by royalty. She sure is pretty." He sounded wistful, as if he had already decided he'd never have a chance with someone so attractive.

Susannah wondered, Doesn't Jeremy know that he's attractive, too? Is that what happens to someone when their mother walks out on them? They think there must be all kinds of things wrong with them, or she wouldn't have left?

Susannah had never met Mrs. Barlow. But seeing the look on Jeremy's face, like a kid looking in the window of a candy store and knowing he couldn't have any, she decided she didn't like Jeremy's mother very much. Jeremy wasn't the most fun person she'd ever met, or the smartest or kindest, but he wasn't a bad person. His mother had hurt him. Maybe permanently.

"Kate," Susannah said then, "your mom will know who's in the VIP suite. We'll ask her."

"That doesn't mean she'll tell us. My-mother-the-head-nurse guards the privacy of patients as if she were the Secret Service protecting the President of the United States."

Susannah nodded. True enough. "What I don't get is why, if this patient wants her identity kept secret, she's holed up in the VIP suite. The press is always on the lookout for someone checking in there. She might as well wave a red flag in front of them."

Kate shrugged. "I guess she wanted the VIP treatment more than she wanted privacy." She let out a small giggle. "Because she thought it included high heels and designer fashions. Boy, was she wrong!" The only designer outfit Kate had ever owned was one she'd received free for modeling in a fashion show held by Susannah's mother to raise money for the new burn unit. She loved the outfit, and she knew she looked good in it. But even if she had the money, it seemed totally stupid to spend hundreds of dollars on clothes when there were so many other places to put money. Like medical school, for instance. Who cared what she wore, anyway? It wasn't as if people walked up to her and asked her how much she'd paid for a sweater or skirt or a pair of jeans. Although, Kate remembered sourly, whenever she wore the designer outfit, Callie Matthews always managed to pop up somewhere to inform everyone in the vicinity that the outfit had been donated. Then Kate had to say sharply, "I *earned* it, Callie, remember?"

Now, she said aloud, "The girl is in a *hospital*. What difference does it make what she's wearing? She can't be expecting visitors if no one is supposed to know she's here."

"She might not even *be* here, at Grant Memorial, long enough for us to find out who she is," Susannah mused aloud. "As soon as they find out what's wrong with her, she'll be carted off on a gurney to one of the other hospitals on the grounds." She smiled. "Or maybe she'll insist on a limo." Her smile widened. "Can't you just see a limo winding its way through one of our covered passageways to the Cardiopulmonary hospital, or to the lab for tests?"

"Personally," Kate said dryly, "my bet is on the Psych building. It sounded to me like the girl could use a few hours on a psychiatrist's couch."

Kate was right about her mother guarding the patient's privacy. All that Astrid Thompson would tell them was, the patient had been experiencing painful, erratic breathing episodes and periods of dizziness, along with severe headaches, and had come to Emsee to find out why. And she told them the girl's name was Emma Slocum.

"No, it's not, Mom," Kate corrected. "It's Amber Taylor. We heard that much."

"And she's beautiful," Jeremy said, awe in his voice.

Astrid fixed dark eyes on her daughter. "Her name," she enunciated carefully, "is Emma Slocum." Her gaze was stern. "I don't have to repeat the rules about not discussing patients outside of this medical facility, do I? Particularly in this case."

"That's not fair!" Kate cried in exasperation. "What does *particularly in this case* mean? You say something like that, and then you wonder why we're curious! What's so special about that girl?"

Lips tightly sealed, Astrid Thompson turned on her heel and went back to her desk.

Outside, a second siren split the air.

"Uh-oh," Kate declared, "what's going on?" She called to her mother, standing behind her desk, "Is something happening at the refinery?"

Nurse Thompson nodded. "There's a fire. But I understood that it was minor. I wonder if that's changed. There shouldn't have been a second siren." Her expression turned grim. "Let's hope there's not a third."

It came, loud and urgent, less than a second later.

Three sirens meant a serious fire.

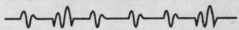

Abby's first thought as Sam pulled the van to a halt just outside the refinery's heavy iron gate was that her anxiety had been unfounded. She saw no bright red fire engines or ambulances anywhere on the site, and no sign that anything was wrong. Her eyes went instantly to the half-dozen fat, black oil tanks clustered off to her right, at the south end of the complex. There was no telltale smoke trailing up toward the cloudless, cobalt-blue sky.

And they hadn't heard more than one siren. But . . . that could have been because Sam's stereo had been blasting during the trip from town.

Before she could allow a deep sigh of relief to escape, her head swiveled to hurriedly survey the buildings and tanks at the north end of the property.

And there it was. Thin, wispy, gray-white, trailing upward, reminding Abby of her grandmother's long, soft hair when, at the end of the day, it was set free of its single braid. Seeing it,

Abby drew her breath in sharply. "Oh, no," she whispered, pointing.

Sam's and Sid's eyes followed her gesture.

A sudden gust of wind attacked the smoke, shredding the plume into feathery wisps. "Jet trail?" Sid asked.

Sam shook his head. "Not on your life. That's a fire." His voice held barely restrained excitement.

Abby heard it, and hated him for it. He wouldn't be excited if there was a chance that *his* father might be somewhere on the refinery grounds. Samuel Grant II owned the Petroleum Products Company, but did he ever go near it? She doubted it. He *paid* people to grub about among the oil tanks. She hadn't run into her best friend's father that often, but when she had, not a single silver-gray hair had been out of place, nor was there so much as a smudge on his expensive cashmere blazers. Any kind of dirt or oil on Samuel Grant II seemed as unlikely as diamonds and mink on Abby O'Connor. Neither would *ever* happen.

A new plume of smoke, this one darker and thicker than the first, began to wend its way skyward.

"Let's go check it out," Sam suggested. "But we're walking the rest of the way. I'll get your chair, Sid. I'm not parking on the grounds. If there *is* a fire, it's not gobbling up my van. Besides, if we leave it out here, it won't be in the way of any fire engines and ambulances."

Abby swallowed hard as she jumped from the van. Ambulances? Her *father* might be inside somewhere.

She still had hope that the plumes of smoke meant nothing. If they did, wouldn't fire trucks already be screaming toward the refinery? The only sound she heard as they hurried inside was the crunching of their shoes and Sid's wheels on the gravel. No sirens.

As they drew closer to the first group of tall, wide, brick office buildings, Sid announced, sounding puzzled, "I don't think that smoke is coming from one of the tanks. I know it should be, but doesn't it look to you like it's a lot closer to one of those buildings?"

They were still some distance away. The refinery site was shaped in a large rectangle, with a cluster of fat tanks at opposite ends on the shorter sides, office buildings and warehouses facing each other along the longer sides. There were thick woods surrounding the site, some of the trees edging the brick buildings.

The building Sid was looking at was at the far end of the site, so close to a group of tanks that Abby found it impossible to tell the source of the smoke. But her heart began pounding wildly. Her father didn't work among the tanks. He worked in an office. In an office *building*. Since she had no idea which one, she didn't want *any* of them to be on fire.

She was as puzzled as Sid. The refinery fires always began in or around the oil tanks, didn't they? Why would an office building be burning?

The closer they got to the smoke, which seemed to be coming thicker and faster now, the more clear it became that the source was not an oil tank. The source was instead a first-floor window of one of the brick buildings. Abby thought she could hear people shouting. It sounded distant, muffled, as if the people were inside a cave or down a well, so she couldn't be sure.

She broke into a run then, her eyes focused on the charcoal-colored smoke. She was almost there, almost to the tall, red brick building spewing smoke, when she heard the first wail of a fire truck, then another, and another. She counted silently as she ran. Three sirens, three trucks. Didn't that mean the fire was serious? As if she couldn't already *tell* that from the smoke pouring not from one window only, she saw now, but from *three* windows. Two on the first floor, one on the second. If her father was in that building, which floor would he be on? If he was on the first or second, he was in terrible danger. And if he was trapped instead on a higher floor, how would he escape?

The muffled shouting sounded louder now. It

was coming from the building that was clearly on fire. There were people inside!

Although Sam and Sid called out to her to wait, and shouted warnings that she shouldn't get too close, Abby kept going, her legs pumping, her breath coming unevenly, as if she had been running for a very long time. But it was anxiety that made her breath short, not exertion. "Which building do you work in, Daddy?" she cried softly as she ran straight toward the brick structure spewing smoke. "Which *one*?"

Will left on the first ambulance dispatched to the refinery from Med Center.

Susannah stopped him before he got to the door. She had heard all three sirens. That meant the fire was a serious one. And Will . . . sweet, funny, stubborn Will was on his way there. That scared her. He knew what he was doing, of course; she was sure of that. He might be the youngest paramedic at Emsee, but he was far from stupid. But she hated it when he went out on fire calls. Everyone knew those calls were the most dangerous. Anything could happen at a fire. The paramedics weren't supposed to go inside, that was up to the firemen. But a paramedic had been seriously injured last spring when the wall of a house collapsed and burning timbers flew every which way. She couldn't stand it if anything like that happened to Will.

She couldn't let him go without saying something to him.

But when she called his name and he stopped and turned around, an expectant look on his face, Susannah was stricken speechless. Exactly what was it she wanted to say? "I don't know what I'd do if something bad happened to you" was too strong. It might scare him. He had never said he felt anything special for her. Abby insisted that he did, and even Kate had hinted as much. But Will hadn't said it. What had they shared, after all? A dance or two, a cup of coffee or two, and a lot of hours volunteering together. She had never been to his house, and he'd never been near Linden Hill unless he was on an ambulance call in the area. He *had* met her parents, during the fever, when Sam had been so ill, but they'd only exchanged a few words. Her mother called him "that nice young African-American who was so concerned about Sam." Will would hate that if he knew, so Susannah hadn't shared that bit of information.

She stood in front of him now, her heart aching with longing, mixed with fear for his safety. His dark eyes were impatient, and she knew he was eager to get going. The ambulance wouldn't wait.

"What?" he prodded gently.

She shook her head, wondering what was in her eyes. How much of what she felt for him showed? And if it was there, would it scare him off? "Just . . . just be careful, okay?" she said lamely, furious with herself for chickening out. "I mean," she added hastily, "if it's a bad fire . . ."

His eyes, which she had, once or twice, seen grow as cold and dark as marbles, were warm, and his smile was the same. "You're worried?" he asked lightly, moving toward her. "About me?"

She should have said yes. That's what she told herself later. She should have answered with an emphatic "Yes, Will, I *am* worried about you." It was the perfect opportunity to stop dancing around the subject of the two of them . . . together . . . and be honest. Like Kate. And Abby. She should have said, "Yes, Will, I am worried about you because I think that you're probably the most important person in my life. At least, I'd like you to be . . . if you want."

She didn't say any of that. She couldn't. She was too afraid he didn't feel the same way. Too afraid that he saw her only as Samuel Grant's daughter. The Rich Girl, that might be how he thought of her. She couldn't stand knowing that. So she said instead, "Well, it's a *fire*, Will. People have to be careful around a fire."

The warmth went from his eyes, and he stopped in his tracks. "Oh, yeah, *people*," he said, his voice cool. Adding brusquely, "Well, don't worry about us *people*, okay? We'll be fine," he hurried away.

If I were double-jointed, Susannah thought as she turned dispiritedly toward the nurses' station, I could kick myself. What is *wrong* with me? I can stand by and hold a suture tray without flinching while people are having their arms and legs sewn back together, I can look at second-degree burns, even third-degree without vomiting like some of the volunteers, and I can see a skull that's been split open in a car crash without fainting. But I can't tell Will Jackson that the thought of something bad happening to him makes me really ill.

She went back to work very angry with herself.

When the wails of the departing vehicles had died down, Astrid handed Susannah a list of supplies. "Fill every cupboard in every trauma and treatment room," she ordered, her voice not quite crisp enough to disguise the tension in it. Head nurse Thompson had worked at Emsee for twenty years, and had seen the worst of the refinery fires. She knew the dry, warm, windy weather could mean disaster, and she knew what to expect if that disaster took place. In spite of many years of nursing, she had never become hardened to the sight of patients with serious burns. Each time she saw one, she visualized the horrors they were going to go through as they healed. If they lived. "Saline, gauze, plenty of both, and alcohol. Get a couple of rolls of disposable sheets, a batch of medical charts, and make absolutely sure we've got more than one crash cart. Borrow a couple from other floors if you have to. Get an orderly to help you."

Susannah ran to obey.

chapter
5

—∿∿∿∿∿∿∿∿—

As she ran, Susannah's stomach churned violently. Crash carts? Astrid was clearly expecting the worst. The equipment the carts contained was used to revive patients who had stopped breathing, for whatever reason: Usually that reason was a heart attack. But sometimes it was a near-drowning incident or a choking episode. Or . . . smoke inhalation.

That's what Astrid is expecting, Susannah realized. If there are people working at the refinery, we could have a lot of cases of smoke inhalation. And smoke kills faster than fire.

How close would Will have to get to that smoke?

She tried to stay optimistic. During her months in Emergency, the staff's record of reviving patients who had stopped breathing had astonished her. Someone would be lying on the table completely limp, without the tiniest sign of life, and minutes later, with the help of CPR and maybe the crash cart, and sometimes the actual opening of the chest in order to stimulate the

44

heart manually, whatever it took, that person eventually began breathing again. Alive again. Amazing!

Susannah ran quickly, gracefully, from one supply closet to the next, rushing up and down staircases rather than waiting for the elevator, her arms filled with medical supplies.

"What's up?" a short, heavyset orderly with unruly red hair called as Susannah dashed past one of the staff lounges.

She struggled to remember his name. Such a huge staff at Emsee, so many people. Joey, that was it, Joey Rudd. "Refinery fire!" she called back, pausing in the hall. "Come and help me dig up a crash cart or two, okay?"

He was next to her in seconds.

"Is somebody out there?" a voice called out as Susannah and the orderly hurried past a room. Susannah didn't realize they were passing the VIP suite until she recognized the voice. It was the new patient. Amber. Or Emma. Whatever her name, there was no mistaking that voice. "Come here, whoever you are! The ice in my water pitcher has melted, and my water is disgustingly warm. I can't be expected to *drink* this. And no one is answering my buzzer. *Why* doesn't this suite have its own fridge?"

Susannah and Joey kept going. She noticed as they passed the semicircular desk in midhall that there were two nurses at the station. One was writing on a patient's medical chart, while the other was talking on the telephone. The light on the computerized board clearly indicated an active buzzer in Suite Four-A, but it was being ignored.

The nurse on the telephone looked up as the two ran past the desk. She covered the mouthpiece with one hand and called out, "You just passed Her Royal Highness's room. What's she want this time? A mink bedspread? Tell her we sent them all out to the furrier to be cleaned."

"Ice!" Susannah called over her shoulder without stopping. "The water in her pitcher is warm." Grinning, she added, "You really should get her a fridge. It'd save you a lot of running back and forth."

The nurse laughed. "Right you are."

Susannah's only thought was to get the crash cart and the supplies down to Emergency as fast as possible. Besides, she was anxious to find out if Will had called in. Then she'd know he was okay. But when she had pressed the elevator button, she couldn't resist taking one last look down the hall toward the VIP suite. Sure enough, she saw a nurse heading for Four-A with a pitcher in hand.

The orderly saw Susannah's quick glance, and nodded. "I don't know who that girl is, but man, she's a royal pain! If I had a dollar for every complaint she's registered since she checked in a couple of hours ago, I'd retire to the Bahamas and live the easy life. Would you believe she kicked up a fuss when she found out the sheets on her bed weren't linen? She claims she's allergic to cotton *and* polyester. Sent her friends out to buy linen sheets, no kidding. Sky blue, she says. She wants sky blue sheets! Said it was her best color. They did it, too. Went right out of here to get what she wanted. Not me. I would have told her to sleep on the floor if she didn't like the sheets."

"I think she's just used to having things her own way," Susannah said as the elevator arrived. "I think she's someone important, so I suppose she's rich."

"Well, *you're* rich," Joey Rudd said staunchly. The door closed upon them. "But you never throw *your* weight around. Everyone thought you would, but . . ." Realizing how that sounded, he reddened and fell silent.

Susannah wasn't offended. On the contrary, Joey's comments meant a lot to her. She wanted more than anything to be accepted at Emsee as just another volunteer. She had tried everything she could think of to get people to relax around her, forget that she was the daughter of the most powerful man in town. All she wanted was to prove that she was willing to work as hard as anyone else. But she could never be sure that anyone noticed. Joey Rudd had, and that was something. If he had, maybe others would, too, and stop treating her differently. *Someday.*

"Thanks, Joey. Our new patient will probably settle down once she's used to the routine. If she's here that long."

Amber Taylor had no intention of remaining at Med Center "that long." She lay in bed in her empty room, picking impatiently at the Purple Pizzazz polish on her nails and lamenting the fact that Nellie, her manicurist, had just phoned to say she wouldn't be making the trip to Med Center after all.

But she *promised*, Amber thought angrily. After I arranged a limo for her! How often does a manicurist get to ride in a limousine? And what excuse had Nellie given? Something lame about another promise, one that involved taking her kids to a children's play.

"On *my* money!" Amber complained aloud. "No one pays Nellie as well as I do, and she knows it. What am I supposed to do now?" She held her hands up in front of her face, surveying the chipped nails with distaste. "I wonder if this awful little city has a decent manicurist. Probably not."

Her hands dropped to the peach blanket and began playing nervously with the satin binding. She glanced around slowly at the peach walls, the wide-open uncurtained windows allowing in ample sunshine and fresh air, the two comfortable armchairs covered in flowered-print fabric, the large, framed wildflower prints on one wall, the tall cabinet housing a television set and VCR, and the stacks of videos that Jules had brought her.

"I hate it here," she whispered softly. Her lovely face crumpled, and tears slid down her cheeks. "Leo's going to replace me on the show, I know it, I just know it. Then I'll have to go back to Tennessee, to that awful little town and that horrible tiny house, and everyone in town will point at me and call me a failure." She burrowed as deep beneath the covers as she could without messing up her hair, and hissed, "I couldn't *stand* that! Marcia Jessup and Betsy Calendar and Joanie Loomis, all of them staring at me everywhere I went and whispering that I had to come home and live in my stepmother's house because I couldn't hack it in the big city. I'd rather die! If I have to go back there, I hope I *am* sick enough to die!"

She was already beginning to dream about her own funeral and how everyone in the business would flock to it because she had died so young, when she drifted off into a discontented, light sleep. Maybe everyone from Nag's Hollow, Tennessee, would charter buses to make the trip to the big city to say good-bye to one of their own who had made it big. Wouldn't that be something? The media would have a field day. The one thing she couldn't decide was which picture she should tell Jules to release with her obituary. Maybe the one with her hair up. It was more sophisticated. Although Bess had always said the one in the scoop-necked red velvet was the best. Maybe that one . . .

When her agent and manager returned to the room carrying the requested sky blue linen sheets, Styrofoam containers filled with the fettuccini Alfredo and Caesar salad, and half a dozen other sundries Amber had asked for, their charge seemed to be sound asleep. Her hair was perfectly arranged around her face, and only the merest hint of tear-streaked mascara stained one perfectly sculpted cheekbone.

The agent reached into a large pink bag and withdrew two fashion magazines, a tiny glass bottle with a stopper, a package of emery boards, a paperback novel, and two bars of scented bath soap. She placed all of the items on Amber's tray table and said with concern, "She's been crying."

"Probably chipped a fingernail." The business manager sounded unconcerned.

"Don't be so hard on her. She's terrified. Scared to death that Leo will replace her."

"She *should* be scared." Jules opened a Styrofoam container, pulled out a carrot stick, and began munching on it. "I've got more hair than Leo has patience." Jules was seriously balding. "He won't wait forever. If they don't figure out what's wrong with this girl and fix it fast, she'll be on a bus back to Georgia or wherever it is she came from faster than you can say 'soap stars are a dime a dozen in New York City.' "

"Tennessee." The tall, attractive woman slid out of her suede coat and draped it carelessly over a chair. "She comes from Tennessee, Jules. And she's not just a pretty face. She's very good at what she does. It's not her fault she's sick. Leo will just *have* to be patient, that's all."

"Ha! When ants dance. You ask me, this girl here would be smart to find herself a rich doctor while she's here. Get married, buy a house, have a couple of kids. She'd be better off."

Amber, not as sound asleep as she appeared to be, heard the remark and tucked it away in the back of her mind for future reference. Because she realized, with a sinking of her heart, that if the doctors here weren't as fast as everyone said, and Leo got tired of waiting and replaced her, she just might have to think seriously about Jules's suggestion.

At the refinery, three fire trucks careened, one after the other, through the open metal gate and raced toward the burning building. The office windows that had been opened to welcome the day's warmth and the autumn breeze were filled now with smoke and darting scarlet flames.

When the trucks screeched to a halt, a fireman ordered Sam, Abby, and Sid away from the scene. They moved to the opposite side of the courtyard and leaned against the wall of a stone warehouse. From there, they watched as firemen hurried to unroll hoses.

"There can't be that many people inside," Sid said. "It's Saturday."

"People work on Saturday sometimes," Abby reminded him. She had already explained her reason for rushing ahead of Sam and Sid. Sam had said, "If you're not sure he's here, why get all bent out of shape about it? Call your house and find out." But Sid had taken Abby's hand and held it tightly in his.

She was about to go in search of a telephone when firemen in yellow rubber slickers and black helmets began leading people from the burning building in groups of two and three. They all had their hands over their mouths, trying to protect their lungs. Many of them were shaking, and their eyes were tearing from the smoke.

Abby scanned every small group for her father. "It looks like lots of people were working. So my dad could have been in there, too. I've got to call home and find out."

But she stayed where she was, keeping her eyes on the burning building. There was more reddish-orange mixed in with the thick, gray smoke now, as firemen unfurled a second fat, white hose and hooked it up to a squat, yellow hydrant. Although Abby watched steadily until the rush of people had dwindled to one or two stragglers staggering through the doorway on the arm of a fireman, there was no sign of her father.

She waited for the expected wash of relief. He hadn't come out of the building. Didn't that mean he hadn't been inside? He hadn't come in to work, after all. He was probably home washing the car or painting that wall in the family room that her baby sister, Toothless, had colored with purple Magic Marker, or maybe he was working or reading in his den. She would call home and he would answer in his deep, jovial voice, saying something idiotic like, "Fulton's Fish Market, salmon on special today," or, "Tony's Pool Hall, no one under eighteen allowed." So juvenile, but her friends loved it. He always answered the phone on weekends, taking the portable if he went outside. Her mother was so busy with the kids, her father laughingly called answering the phone "helping out."

Abby spotted a pay phone stationed on a wall two buildings away. Telling Sid and Sam she'd be right back, she hurried over to it. A wave of smoke caught her in the face, making her eyes tear, burning her throat. She slid the quarter into the slot and dialed.

It was ringing on the other end when one of the evacuees called to a fireman in a hoarse voice, "That building isn't empty! There are still people inside! A wall blew, and some people went down.

I don't know who was involved, but there was so much smoke, we couldn't see to get them out. You have to go in and find them."

Abby heard every word. Her breath quickened in her throat. Her heart was racing. But she told herself that any second now, her father's voice would say, "Fulton's Fish Market . . ."

"Hello?"

Her mother's voice. Not her father's. Her mother's.

There was only one reason her father wouldn't be answering the phone on Saturday.

He wasn't home.

chapter
6

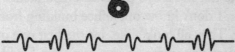

"**M**om?" Abby managed, willing her voice to remain steady. "Is Dad there?" Behind her, another siren sounded. She turned her head to see all three of the ambulances pull away from the site and race through the iron gate. The speed at which the vehicles took off, their wheels spinning in the gravel, surprised her. None of the people escaping the building had seemed injured. But then, she reminded herself, you couldn't *see* smoke-damaged lungs.

"Mom?" Why hadn't her mother answered? "Didn't you hear me?"

"Abby? Is that you? There's so much noise . . . where are you?"

"At the refinery. There's a fire. Put Dad on, okay?"

"I heard the whistle. But it's not bad, is it? The fire? One of the tanks, I guess?"

"No, that's the weird thing. It's an office building this time." Abby was about to scream with the need to hear her father's voice. "And I can't tell how bad it is. People were inside . . ."

Her mother's gasp interrupted Abby. "Office building?" Charlie O'Connor's voice sharpened. "*Which* office building?"

The last of Abby's patience evaporated. "God, Mom, I don't know one office building from the other. They all look alike. It's the first one on the left after you come in the gate. Put Daddy on, and I'll ask him which building that is."

There was a moment or two of maddening silence before Abby heard, "Honey, he's not here. He . . . he had to go in to work this morning."

Abby clutched the receiver. She'd been right. He *had* said something last night about working this morning. "Which building does he work in, Mom?" Her father had never taken her to see where he worked, although she'd asked more than once. He'd said the refinery was no place for a child. "Which *one*, Mom?"

Her mother's voice sank to a whisper. "I don't know, Abby. He works in Engineering, but I don't know which building that is." There was urgency in her voice as she added, "*Ask* someone. Now! Ask someone which building is on fire."

Abby turned. And gasped in shock as she saw how thoroughly consumed by flames the building had become. Tall spires of flames stretched greedily toward the branches of the tall, old trees surrounding the complex. Abby's gaze moved quickly to the letters over the door. Thick, black smoke blocked out part of the word. But she was able to see an *N* and a *G* and an *I*, then, as a wave of smoke dissipated for a second, another *N* and two *E*'s. The smoke thickened again, but not before she had deciphered an *ING* ending.

Sick at heart, she staggered back against the brick wall, struggling to compose herself. When she had taken several deep breaths, she reluctantly spoke into the receiver again. "I don't need to ask," she told her mother. "I can see the letters over the door. The building that's on fire is Engineering."

"I'll be right there," Charlie O'Connor said hastily, and hung up.

The click of the receiver left Abby feeling lost and alone.

At Med Center, the staff had been alerted both to the refinery fire and to incoming patients in multiple ambulances. The word they'd received in advance was that there were no burns involved, but varying degrees of smoke inhalation damage. Some cases had been reported by the paramedics as severe.

Orderlies ran through the halls armed with oxygen tanks, depositing their cargo in treatment and trauma rooms.

Two hyperbaric decompression chambers were ready to receive any patients whose carbon monoxide poisoning was high enough to warrant one hundred percent oxygen at increased atmospheric pressure. In the chambers, the life-saving oxygen entered the bloodstream at a faster rate. The chambers saved lives. Patients who were not as ill would be given oxygen by mask.

"How many?" Kate had heard her mother asking Will when he called in on the radio to give their estimated arrival time at three minutes. Then she'd heard, "Thirteen? All at the same time? Okay, we're ready."

They *were* ready, though thirteen patients was a lot at one time. They'd had worse, even in the short time since Kate and Susannah had come onboard. The awful fever that had swept through town earlier in the year had been devastating. Still, those patients hadn't come in all at the same time. Emsee's emergency facilities had been stretched tighter during the last flood, when patients had been brought in in multiples, sometimes as many as two dozen at a time.

But the staff had handled it all with speed and competency. And, Kate felt, with compassion. And though she was anxious, she knew they'd handle this newest emergency the same way.

The ambulances arrived one right after the other with shrieking brakes. Staff members, including Kate and Susannah, were waiting at the emergency entrance.

The damage was extensive. Without exception, the patients' eyes were red and raw. Their faces were gray with smoke, and shock. An eye doctor was summoned from upstairs for the more serious cases, as a precautionary measure, though none of the patients had suffered eye burns.

The degree of carbon monoxide poisoning varied. Kate knew the deadly poison, even if it didn't kill, would continue to wreak havoc until it had been completely eliminated from bloodstreams. But the treatment and trauma rooms had been well-supplied with oxygen tanks and masks. The head nurse knew what she was doing.

The first two women to arrive were disoriented, no longer sure who or where they were. They were suffering from severe nausea, and vomiting. But they were conscious.

They were rushed to trauma rooms to be examined for lung damage. Even if it wasn't serious, Kate knew they wouldn't be released that same day. When the nausea had been brought under control with medication, the women would be admitted and watched for signs of pneumonia, bronchitis, and other complications from smoke damage.

Behind them, a trio of men in business suits had the same symptoms, but suffered the additional problem of muscle weakness. When they made a valiant effort to walk, their legs folded beneath them and they sank to the ground. They were terrified by this new sign of physical damage, and would have panicked if Will hadn't been there to talk to them in a soothing, calm voice. Susannah watched with admiration. Paramedics helped the men into wheelchairs and hurried them off to receive the necessary oxygen.

A man and a woman, who Kate later learned were husband and wife, couldn't remember their own names or each other's. The woman kept murmuring in agitation, "What's wrong with me, what's wrong with me?" Kate assured her she would be fine, that the condition was only temporary, but the woman either didn't hear her or didn't have any idea what "condition" Kate was talking about. She continued to murmur as she was led away.

The woman who arrived directly behind them repeatedly cried that she couldn't see properly, although there was no sign that she had been burned. She was terrified that the blindness was permanent, and hysterical as a result of her fear. Will, wheeling her to an examination room, tried to calm her down, but she was crying too loudly to hear his voice.

The last four patients to arrive were unconscious and in critical condition. Following the fastest preliminary examination Susannah had ever seen, they were all rushed directly to the decompression chambers.

It seemed to Kate and Susannah that there

were patients everywhere, in exam rooms, in trauma and treatment rooms. Fortunately, they'd had time to prepare. A call for "all staff to emergency" brought enough doctors and nurses to handle the situation.

"What I hate about smoke inhalation victims," Kate said when she and Susannah had done all they could to help, "is that we don't know right away that they're really okay. I mean, if a leg is broken, a doctor sets it and we know it will heal. If someone comes in with a heart attack and the doctors revive him, he's scheduled for surgery and we know *that* will probably heal him. But with smoke damage, even if they seem okay when they leave here and are taken upstairs, they might develop pneumonia or bronchitis or edema. It's going to be hard to keep up with all these people," she said, waving a hand toward the treatment room they'd just left. "To find out for sure that they all made it okay."

At least, Susannah told herself, I know now that Will is okay. For now. He came back from the fire this time unhurt. She found herself wishing with all her heart that he wouldn't have to go back there. But she knew he'd go even if someone told him he didn't have to. Because that's who he was. If he could help, he'd be there.

Word of the refinery fire had begun to spread. The waiting room, as it always did during a medical crisis, began to fill with relatives and friends of refinery workers. Kate was grateful that since it was a Saturday, the site had not been fully occupied, which kept the crowd down. But it soon became clear that there had been quite a few people working overtime on this weekend, because nearly every blue plastic bench and yellow chair was filled.

Since the staff had its hands full treating the injured, Susannah and Kate took on the task of soothing frightened relatives and handing out coffee and magazines. They did all they could to keep everyone inside the waiting room and out of the busy corridors, where they would interfere with rushing wheelchairs and gurneys.

The news began to circulate that except for one minor searing of an ear, no one had been burned.

"Yet," Astrid said grimly as she finished filling out a medical chart. "This isn't over yet, kiddies. In fact, if what I've heard is true, it's just beginning."

The last patient was a young fireman whose only symptom was wheezing and coughing. His eyes, too, were red and raw, but he was otherwise intact. "I had a mask on," he gasped as Kate helped him into a wheelchair. He was still wearing his black protective helmet, and his face was hidden behind a thick layer of soot and grime.

"It's a mess over there," he choked as he settled into the wheelchair. Kate moved quickly behind the chair to hurry him inside. "It's wild, man! The way the wind is whipping that fire around, we'll be lucky if the whole refinery doesn't go up in smoke. Not to mention the whole city. That building that's burning now, it's surrounded by trees, you know what I'm saying? They've all still got their leaves, nice and dry, like tinder at a campfire." He shook his head. "This one's going to be bad, man, really bad."

Although she never slowed her steps, Kate's hands tightened on the wheelchair handles. The refinery was in Eastridge. So was her home, the small, neat house where she lived with her parents and her younger brother, Aaron. They'd come close to losing it in that last flood. Had it survived only to be consumed by flames now?

"They'll put the fire out," she said with far more confidence than she felt. "They always do. Maybe the wind will die down."

The young fireman shook his head a second time. "I don't *think* so. I checked with the weather station. The captain asked me to. The guy over there said high winds are predicted for the next forty-eight hours at least."

"They've been wrong before," Kate said irritably. She admired firemen, risking their lives the way they did, but did he *have* to be giving her all this bad news? She had work to do here, plenty of it, judging by the way things were going. How could she concentrate if she was worried about the fire?

And she *was* worried about the fire.

It seemed to her that everyone should be.

chapter
7

—◊◊◊◊◊◊◊—

Kate felt a little guilty when she arrived at the trauma center to see so much activity inside the rooms, when all she was doing was helping the barely injured fireman. But, she told herself defensively, he needed help, too. He was anxious to get back to work, and he couldn't do that until he'd been thoroughly checked out to see what kind of treatment, if any, he needed.

Because he was not seriously injured, he had to wait, his wheelchair parked outside a busy trauma room where doctors were still working on one of the women battling fierce nausea. Kate went to get the fireman a cold drink, and a wet cloth to soothe his sore eyes and wipe the thick layer of charcoal soot off his face.

When he had done the latter, and Kate got a good look at him, her jaw dropped. "Damon?"

He looked up, the cloth in his hands. "Hi, there, Katie. Thought that was you. You scooted behind my chair so fast, didn't get a good look at your face. How you doin'?"

Kate stared at him in disbelief. "You're a fireman?" She was stunned. Damon Lawrence had been one of Will's best friends for years, until Damon dropped out of high school. He'd been one of the victims of the fever that had swept the city during the summer. She'd sat by his bed more than once, mostly because there wasn't anyone else to do it. He had come very close to dying. Before that, the last she'd heard of him was that he was working split shift at the refinery and, as far as she was concerned, going nowhere fast. Now he was a fireman? "Since when have you been fighting fires?"

"Since August. I got my GED this past spring. Then I didn't know what to do with it. While I was getting better in the hospital this summer, I had lots of time to think. I figured refinery work just wasn't gonna cut it, so I applied at the fire department. Aced the course, by the way," he added with a confident grin. "So here I am, riskin' life and limb to protect the fine citizens of this here fair city." His grin widened. "So what do ya think, Katie, am I a respectable member of society now or what?"

"Don't call me Katie! I hate it." Will must not have known about this new career of Damon's. He would have told her. "I saw you this summer, Damon. You offered me a ride at the bus stop, remember? Right about the time the fever broke out here. You didn't say anything then about getting your GED or becoming a fireman."

He sipped the water she'd brought him. When he lifted his head, his dark eyes seemed to look right through her. "I remember all right. You didn't give me the chance to tell you nothin'."

Kate flushed, remembering. She had turned down the ride and told him he was stupid for quitting school. Still, he could have said, "For your information, Miss High-and-Mighty, I've got my GED and I'm goin' somewhere." He hadn't said that. That wasn't *her* fault.

There was activity all around them. Staff members rushed back and forth with people who had been treated and were being released, with others who were being admitted for further observation, and with still others lying on gurneys on their way to the Cardiopulmonary hospital on the grounds for more intensive treatment. Kate, flustered by the awkward situation with Damon, glanced up and saw Jeremy's father, Chief Cardiologist Dr. Thomas Barlow, striding confidently toward a trauma room. The inhalation of smoke, she decided, must have either created a heart problem, or aggravated an existing condition. If anyone could take care of a cardiac problem, it was Jeremy's father.

Susannah, her arms filled with linens, hurried down the hall toward them. Kate, finding herself suddenly anxious to escape Damon's dark, penetrating eyes, called out, "Need me?" It wasn't as if he was seriously ill. There wasn't any reason why he couldn't wait alone for his treatment.

But Susannah shook her head. "No. It may not look like it," she said, glancing around at the corridor busy with staff, wheelchairs, and gurneys, "but everything's under control. You take care of the fireman. He's important."

"Hey, you hear that?" Damon asked, grinning up at Kate. "I know who that is. That girl, she's a Grant. Daughter of The Great Man himself. She says I'm important, then that's what I am. So you better treat me right, Katie."

Jeremy poked his head around a corner. "You seen my dad?" he asked Kate.

She nodded. "He's busy. You want to wait for him here?" She hoped he'd say yes. It was weird, how uncomfortable she felt around Damon. What was *that* all about? She'd known Damon Lawrence practically all of her life. They'd played together as kids in Eastridge. When she was eleven, she had thought maybe she'd marry him someday, just like every other girl in the neighborhood who knew him. Now, all of a sudden she felt jittery around him? Why?

Because, a stern voice answered her, when he dropped out of school, didn't you think, just a little bit, that you were better than him? Because you were going into medicine and Damon wasn't going into anything? That's how you saw it. And seeing it that way set you miles apart. Now that he's pulled his life together, you're equals. That means there's no distance between you. The truth is, Damon makes you nervous because by pulling his life together, he's taken away your excuse for keeping him out of your life. And you're scared to death of what will happen if you let him back in.

Ridiculous! Kate snapped back silently, even as she found herself backing away from Damon's wheelchair to lean against the corridor wall opposite him. I'm only interested in him as a patient, just like every other patient who comes in here, that's all.

Why was he smiling at her like that? As if he knew a secret. As if he'd heard the little voice in her head, heard every word. But of course he couldn't have. He didn't know anything about her, not anymore. They weren't kids now. She'd changed. A lot. Damon didn't have a clue about who she was these days.

So why was he smiling?

At the refinery, a sudden gust of wind yanked the flames out of the upper stories of the burning building and flung them into the treetops. The hot, reaching fingers curled around the crisp, dry leaves, and squeezed. The branches exploded in clouds of vivid red and yellow and orange.

On the ground below, Sid said from his wheelchair, "Uh-oh, did you see *that*? Looks like it's getting away from them. They're watering down the tanks, but that might not be enough."

He, Abby, and Sam hadn't moved from their spot against the wall of the building opposite the fire scene. They had been joined by a group of refinery employees in gray work clothes and boots. A few clutched black metal lunch boxes. All of the faces, some young, some not so young, were anxious, their eyes now on the blazing trees behind the building.

"That's all she wrote," one of the older workers, a woman, said with grim resignation. "That fire's gonna jump from tree to tree all the way to the woods, you mark my words. Once it hits the woods, there's no stoppin' it. Don't even matter now if the tanks don't blow. That fire's on its way to town."

Nodding agreement, a young man in a yellow hard hat said, "It's not the fire department's fault. It's the wind. Even if they do get the fire out, the wind could just whip the embers back into an inferno again."

Under his breath, Sid muttered to Sam, "And you thought *I* was being pessimistic?"

All three ambulances returned, just ahead of Abby's mother, who rushed onto the scene in jeans and a Grant University sweatshirt, her hair carelessly topknotted, her face putty-colored. "I had to park outside the gate," she gasped, clutching Abby's arm. "I got here as fast as I could. I left Geneva in charge of the kids. God only knows whether or not the house will still be standing when I get back home. Have you seen your father? Where is he?"

Abby fought back tears. "I don't know. He . . . he hasn't come out yet."

Charlie O'Conner whirled around to stare at the flaming building. "Oh, he's not in *there*, Abby, you can't mean he's in *there*!"

Abby hastened to add, "Maybe he isn't, Mom. I mean, he could have gone somewhere else on the site, to one of the tanks, maybe, or he could be eating lunch in another building. He could be anywhere." What she didn't add was, if her father *was* somewhere else on the site, why hadn't he come to watch the fire, along with everyone else?

Two firemen staggered out of the building, their hands to their masked faces, and were taken straight to one of the waiting ambulances.

Seeing the firemen, Abby's mother broke away from the crowd of onlookers and ran to the back of the ambulance. Abby followed.

"There isn't anyone left in the building, is there?" Mrs. O'Connor asked the choking, gasping firemen sitting inside the ambulance clutching oxygen masks. "You made sure it was empty, right?"

Unable to talk, they shook their heads negatively.

Abby wasn't sure what that meant. Did it mean they hadn't been able to make sure the building was empty? Or did it mean there was no one left in there?

Mother and daughter waited in agitation until one of the firemen removed his oxygen mask and croaked, "Dunno. Still checking. Don't think anyone's left in there, though. You'd better get back now. The way the wind's whipping that smoke around, you could end up in here with us."

"I'm not going anywhere," Charlie O'Connor said emphatically, "until I know that building is empty."

Hearing the determination in her voice, no one argued with her. Mother and daughter leaned against the open ambulance door, keeping their anxious eyes on the burning building.

In the VIP suite at Grant Memorial, Amber Taylor waited for a handsome young doctor to walk into her room. The way she saw it, it might be the only way out for her. She had called Leo in New York, tried to make him think she was practically on her way home right now. But he wasn't buying.

"I just talked to Bess thirty minutes ago," he'd said, his voice cool. "She said you haven't even been checked out yet, Amber. Don't try and do a number on me, kiddo. It won't work."

She hadn't given up. "A friend brought me a magazine," she tried, carefully keeping desperation out of her voice. "There's an article in here about *me*, can you believe it? The writer says such nice things about me, about how no one else in the world could do what I do, as well as I do it. Isn't that wonderful? I'll send you a copy." She wouldn't, because there was no magazine, and no article. But Leo would forget she'd offered, anyway. All she was interested in doing now was reminding him how important she was. In case he was already forgetting.

"Yeah, you do that. Look, I gotta run. Get better, okay?" Click.

Tears of fury and a certain amount of fear stung Amber's eyes. How dare he dismiss her like that? Like flicking a mosquito off his arm! After all she'd done for him. Everyone said so, everyone said that Leo was sinking fast until Amber showed up and breathed new life into his career. Well, practically everyone.

A technician dressed in white, with a carryall full of plastic vials over one wrist, walked briskly into the room.

"What *is* all that noise out there?" Amber demanded. "All those sirens, they're making me crazy. I don't know how you expect me to get any rest in this place."

"There's a fire," the technician answered. She pulled a piece of rubber tubing out of her case and tied it around Amber's upper arm. Then she plucked a syringe free and aimed it at Amber. "At the refinery, on the other side of town. Don't worry, you're safe enough here."

"A fire?" Amber thought of her face. Her fortune. Her face was her fortune, or so her stepmother had said ten zillion times before Amber left for New York. "Anything happens to that," Claire had said coldly, "you're in deep trouble, girl. Better stay out of the sun." Flames from a fire would be worse than the sun. Much worse. "How bad is it? The fire."

The technician shrugged. She swabbed Amber's arm with a wet cotton ball. "Bad, I guess. Judging by what I saw in ER a little while ago. The place was jammed. Mostly smoke damage, I think. Didn't see any burn victims."

Amber shuddered, and the needle slipped and scratched her skin. When she yelped in pain, the technician apologized and remedied the situation by inserting the needle properly. It still hurt.

But Amber was too worried about the fire to complain about having blood taken from her arm. After all, her arm wasn't her *fortune*.

"Are you positive," she asked the technician, "that the fire won't come here?"

chapter
8

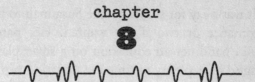

"**Y**ou're not going back to the fire, are you?" Kate asked Damon when he sat up on the examination table.

He had been checked out by one of the residents, given oxygen, and pronounced physically fit. No lung involvement, no carbon monoxide poisoning. His only injury seemed to be a minor burn on his left hand. Kate had applied the salve herself, while Damon joked about how long he'd been waiting for the chance to hold her hand.

Kate was certain it was her imagination that had tricked her into thinking she'd actually felt a jolt of electricity when she took his hand in hers, as if Damon were holding a live wire in his other hand. Ridiculous. Guys *never* affected her that way. Sure, she liked to date, to dance, to have fun.

But she had plans, and it was going to take a lot of time and a lot of hard work to fulfill those plans. She didn't need any distractions, like some stupid romantic involvement. Two of the girls she'd gone to grade school with were already married. One had a kid. She wasn't going that route.

It was okay for someone like Susannah to have a romance or two if she wanted. Her parents would hand her an education on a silver platter, so she'd have plenty of time for a relationship . . . if Will ever swallowed his pride and admitted how he felt about Susannah, which he probably never would. But if he did, Susannah would have time for him.

School wasn't going to be such an easy ride for Kate Thompson. She'd have to work her way through. Med school all by itself was rough, everyone said so. Interns and residents complained about it all the time. They were constantly warning off the volunteers who expressed any interest in medicine, telling them to steer clear of the field unless they wanted to "grow old real fast."

So the last thing in the world Kate Thompson needed was a guy in her life to distract her. She *had* imagined the tingling sensation. And that look of amusement on Damon's very gorgeous face did *not* mean that he'd felt something, too.

"You see this coat?" he asked, shrugging into the yellow rubber slicker. "This here is a fireman's coat, Katie. You think I'm wearin' it just to impress people? Like I ever cared about impressing people. I wear it because I'm a fireman now, and that means I gotta be where the fire is, right?"

She didn't want him to go back there. Didn't want him to leave at all. That annoyed her so deeply, her voice sharpened considerably. "There are *other* firemen. You're not indispensable, Damon. You haven't rested long enough, not yet."

He reached down to pick up his black helmet. Fixing his dark eyes on hers, he asked, "You worried about me, Katie?" And although his tone was light, the look in his eyes was serious.

That scared her. "Oh, forget it!" she snapped, turning away from him.

He put out a hand and caught her by the elbow to stop her from turning away. "Look at me, Kate."

Lifting her chin defiantly, she looked.

When he saw the expression on her face, he said softly, "Well, how *about* that? You *are* shook. Over *me*."

Kate yanked her elbow free, but not before she'd felt that same tingling sensation from his hand on her arm. "I'm shook up about the *fire*!" she insisted, more loudly than she'd planned. "The thought of a refinery fire freaks me out, okay? Just like it would anyone with half a brain."

He astonished her then, by raising his hand to quickly, gently, slide it along her cheek. At the same time, he said in that same, gentle voice,

"Hey, don't worry, okay? We'll handle the fire. You just take care of things here. I'll touch base with you later, when I find out how things are going."

That was nice of him. Very thoughtful, not wanting her to worry. He'd probably do the same for anyone worried about the fire. Susannah or Abby or Will. Anyone. Probably.

Kate took a step backward, away from his hand. "Thanks." Then she added quickly, "Because we'll need to know what's happening out there at the refinery. The staff will, I mean. So we can be ready if there's any more incoming." As if they didn't both know the hospital would be kept up-to-date by any paramedics on the scene.

"Yeah, sure." He plopped the black helmet on his head and, waving casually, said, "So, maybe I'll see you later?"

She nodded, and thawed enough to add, "Be careful, okay?"

His back already to her, he shrugged and walked away, his long legs taking huge strides in his hurry to return to the fire.

Kate watched until he'd rounded a corner and disappeared from sight.

When the last of the smoke inhalation patients had been treated and either released or admitted, the staff returned to the business of treating the remaining Saturday patients in the waiting room. Susannah was so busy keeping the treatment and trauma rooms supplied with gauze and alcohol and disposable sheets, she wasn't aware that Will had returned to the hospital until she bumped into him in the hall as she moved from one room to another.

She had just taken a fresh suture tray to a resident assigned to stitch up the leg of a three-year-old who had been tap-dancing on a glass coffee table, when she saw Will standing in the doorway of a staff lounge, sipping from a Styrofoam cup.

She went over to him, remarking with concern, "You look tired." Will was usually so energetic, loping along the halls with long, brisk strides. That was one of the things that had caught her attention when she'd first met him. But now his shoulders were slightly slumped, and his expression was grim.

"Just brought a fireman in," he said, leaning against the door frame. "A burning beam fell on him. Our first burn case." He inclined his head. "Took him to trauma room five. Izbecki's with him, and they're calling in someone from the burn unit."

"Is it bad?" Susannah asked.

He nodded. "Pretty gruesome. Looked to me like third-degree, at least on his legs. He had gear on. It helped, but not much." Will paused, then added, "They think there might still be people inside the building."

Will sounded so tentative that Susannah glanced at him sharply. When he avoided her eyes, uneasiness stirred within her. "Will?" She moved closer, peering up into his eyes. "Something's going on. What is it? What's wrong?"

Shifting uncomfortably, he answered, "Look, it's probably nothing. I mean, I don't *know* that it's anything. No one does. But . . ."

"Will! Just *tell* me!"

"Okay, okay. Abby's out there, at the fire."

Susannah's heart lurched. "Abby?"

"She and her mother. Her father went to work today. He doesn't usually work on Saturdays, I guess, but he had something he had to finish. The thing is" — Will shifted again, and refused to look at Susannah — "the thing is, he works in that building that's on fire. The Engineering building. And he hasn't shown up anywhere else yet. So . . . so there's a possibility that he's still inside."

Susannah felt sick. She swallowed hard. Abby's father? In that fire, the fire that had seared the lungs of more than a dozen people and felled a fireman with a blazing beam?

Images of her frequent visits to the O'Connor house, where she was more comfortable than she had ever been in her luxurious three-room suite on the second floor of Linden Hall, flashed into her mind. Mr. O'Connor wrestling on the family room floor with four-year-old Mattie, his only son. Rocking two-year-old Toothless when she was crying because of an earache. Charlie O'Connor playing holiday songs on the piano while her husband bellowed the words in his rich Irish tenor. The entire family playing touch football on the lawn and letting Susannah play, too, even though she had known next to nothing about any sport that didn't involve membership in a country club. She did now, though. Brendan and Charlie O'Connor had taught her.

Most of all, Susannah thought of the way Abby hugged her father good night, always, before she left the house in the evening.

"Abby's father?" Susannah finally managed. "Missing?"

Will shrugged. "Maybe not. We're not sure yet. But all of the other refinery workers are on the scene. Someone said a wall blew, and they thought part of it hit him and he went down. No one's positive that's what happened. But the thing is, O'Connor doesn't seem to be around anywhere. The firemen keep going back in, looking for him, but the heat and smoke are so intense, they can't stay in there more than a few minutes."

When Susannah didn't say anything, Will added, "I just found out that one of the firefighters is a friend of mine, or used to be, anyway. Damon Lawrence. We were tight the whole time we were growing up. Then we kind of lost touch.

I didn't even know he'd become a fireman." Will smiled. "One of the other guys said Damon's a real hot dog. In such a big hurry to prove he can do the job, he's not as careful as he's supposed to be. Breaking a few rules, is my guess. Hasn't changed much. He was always like that."

Susannah wasn't listening. "I should go over there," she said quietly. "I should be there for Abby. She'd be there for me. But" — she glanced around the still-crowded waiting room and halls — "I might be needed here." Pain in her eyes, she thought for a minute, then added slowly, "I don't know what to do."

"I think you should stay here." Will moved to put an arm around her shoulders, pulling her close to him. An orderly passing by with an empty gurney grinned at them. "Abby's mom is with her," Will said, "and Sam and Sid. And you're right. Since the fire has already spread to the trees and it's threatening the tanks, we know this is going to be a big one, Susannah. The smoke victims were just the beginning. You *will* be needed here. Abby would understand."

Susannah let her cheek rest against Will's chest. Poor Abby. The not knowing would be the worst part. How could the O'Connor family stand the waiting?

Susannah knew Sam would, in spite of the terror of the situation, manage to find *some* humor somewhere, might even manage to pull a smile out of Abby while they waited. And Sid, an expert on pain himself, would, in only a few words, let Abby know he understood what she was going through. Sid was good at that. Charlie O'Connor, no matter how frantic with worry she was about her husband, would hold Abby close, comforting her. They would comfort each other.

"Okay," Susannah said reluctantly, pulling away from Will, "you're right. *I'm* right. I'll be needed here. Abby will understand. But let me know the very second you hear anything about her father, okay? You can call in on the radio."

The PA system announced an ambulance run, back to the fire site, and Will snapped to attention. Before he hurried away, Susannah echoed softly Kate's earlier admonition to Damon, "You be careful, okay?"

And like Damon, Will nodded and waved, then hurried away. He looked less fatigued than he had a few minutes earlier.

The orderly who had witnessed the hug passed by, and smiled at Susannah. "Nothin' like a hug from a pretty girl to pick up a guy's spirits. Jackson's got a real bounce to his steps now."

Susannah was too worried about Abby's father, and about the fire, to return the smile.

Needing to keep busy, she turned and went back to the suture room to hold the hand of the little tap dancer.

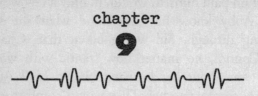

Jeremy couldn't believe what he was doing. It wasn't like him to poke his nose in where it might not be wanted. But he couldn't help it. Ever since he'd seen that gorgeous face in the VIP suite, all he could think about was seeing it again. With everyone in the hospital caught up in the refinery fire, this might be his best chance to sneak into the suite unnoticed. If he got caught, he'd just say he was looking for his father.

Anyway, it wasn't like he was breaking into the suite. The door was ajar. He simply stepped over the threshold and when the girl in the bed looked up, he said, "Hi." He didn't see anyone else in the room. It sure was fancy. Not like any of the other hospital rooms he'd seen. She must be someone really important.

"I thought maybe you could use a friend," he said boldly, surprising himself. "I guess being in the hospital isn't much fun, right?" He'd never been a patient. But he could imagine what it must be like. There couldn't be that much difference between being in the hospital all alone and being at home all alone, could there? He knew what *that* was like, ever since his mother had taken off for San Francisco. She kept inviting him to come and live with her, but he wasn't good enough at making friends to leave the place he'd lived in all his life.

The girl in the bed smiled at him. Jeremy's knees puddled. He had never seen anyone so attractive, not even Susannah, who was pretty, or Kate, who looked like a model, or Abby, who was really cute. This girl in the bed was as close to beautiful as Jeremy had ever seen.

"Hi," she said, still smiling. Her voice was husky, sexy, just as Jeremy had known it would be. "Are you a doctor?"

She thought he looked old enough to be a doctor? Jeremy suddenly felt taller, older, wiser. But he told the truth. "No." Laughing a little self-consciously, he moved on into the room and approached the bed.

She looked disappointed. "Oh. Then what are you doing in my room?"

She wasn't going to make him leave, was she? Before he had a chance to talk to her? He was blowing this before it had even started, just by not being a doctor? Oh, no, no way, that was *not* the way this was going to go. Impulsively, he reached down and lifted one of her incredibly fine-boned wrists, pretending to take her pulse.

"I'm not a doctor," he said, "just an . . . an intern. My chief asked me to look in on you, see how you're doing." The lie came so easily, it astonished him.

The patient glanced suspiciously at Jeremy's red sweater and chinos. "I thought interns dressed in white coats, just like real doctors. And you don't even have a stethoscope hanging around your neck."

Jeremy thought fast. Too late to admit the truth now. "Well, sure. But I . . . I was on my way out of the hospital when Dr. . . . Barlow asked me to look in on you." Good thinking, using his dad's name. That way, if she asked a nurse if there was a Dr. Barlow on staff, the nurse would say yes.

The patient brightened considerably. "You're going to be a doctor?"

Jeremy Barlow would have cut out his own heart before he would even consider going into medicine. After seeing how the profession consumed his father's time, talent, and energy, he knew a hospital was the very last place in the world he would want to spend his own adult years.

But this girl was looking up at him with more interest than he had had the good fortune to see in any other girl's eyes. So he said easily, "Yeah, I am. If," he added hastily, "I pass my boards when the time comes."

"Oh, you will," she said sweetly. "I'm sure you will. You must be very dedicated if you'd take the time to see me when you could be on your way home. What's your name?"

Jeremy thought fast. He only knew one intern, a guy named Ken Noone, who was currently doing six weeks in Cardiology. "Noone," Jeremy said, "Jeremy Noone." Killing two birds with one stone. There *was* an intern named Noone in the hospital, should she ask. At the same time, if one of the staff came into the suite and called him "Jeremy," that would be okay, too. Unless, of course, her medical problem was cardiac in nature, in which case she might very well be staring into the face of the real Dr. Noone any minute now. And that face wouldn't be Jeremy's.

"Well," she said, and he thought for a second that she actually batted her eyelashes at him, although he couldn't be positive, "if you have a minute or two to spare for a poor, ailing patient, why don't you just sit down here and tell me all about yourself?" She waved the delicate wrist toward one of the flowered chairs beside her bed. Her smile widened. "I'm Amber Taylor. Sit, almost-doctor Noone."

Jeremy sat.

Downstairs, a small, pretty, blonde girl in black leggings, an oversized yellow tunic, and high-heeled black boots hurried into Emergency. She ran up to the nurses' desk, where Susannah was anxiously awaiting word from Will about Abby's father, and asked breathlessly, "Where *is* she? Which room is she in?"

Susannah and the head nurse exchanged a blank look. "Where is *who*?" Susannah asked. "Who are you looking for, Callie?"

"*Lynette*, of course," Callie Matthews answered impatiently. The only child of Caleb Matthews, administrator of the Medical Center complex, she was used to having her demands met quickly. "Lynette Martin. She just came in this morning. My friend Edie was here, being treated for a stomachache, she gets them all the time, only I don't think she really has anything wrong with her, she's just trying to get attention, anyway, she was here and she swears she actually saw Lynette being checked in here this morning. So where *is* she?"

"You'd have to check with admitting," Astrid said, "you know that, Callie. Unless this Lynette came in on an emergency basis. And I don't remember any patient by that name coming in here."

"Neither do I," Susannah agreed.

"It wasn't an emergency. And she *did* check in here. Edie said so, and she wouldn't lie. Well, she would, but not about this."

Astrid studied the admitting forms. "Nope,"

she said, shaking her head. "There's no Lynette Martin listed here. Your friend must be mistaken."

Callie clapped a hand to her forehead. "Oh, silly me, what's the matter with my brain? She wouldn't be registered under that name. That's just her name on the *show*." She glanced at Susannah. "You know, the soap opera, *A New Day*. It's on every afternoon at one. You must watch it, Susannah, everyone does. If we can't watch, we tape it." When Susannah continued to look blank, Callie turned back to Astrid. "I can't believe you didn't recognize her when she checked in. She's really famous. She won Most Promising Newcomer this year at the Suds Awards."

Susannah knew, suddenly, exactly who Callie was talking about. An actress. Of course! Why hadn't they guessed? Susannah didn't watch soap operas, but she knew the name Callie was going to say even before Callie's mouth formed the words.

"Amber Taylor, that's her real name," Callie said. "Check your list, see if she's there. I know she is. Amber Taylor."

Astrid gave no sign at all that the name meant anything to her.

"I absolutely *have* to have her autograph," Callie gushed as Astrid pretended to glance over the admitting list again. "Maybe I'll even get some pointers from her on how to become a famous actress. That might be something I'd be interested in after high school. Everyone says I'm pretty enough." With total confidence that her request would be fulfilled, she asked the head nurse, "So? Which room *is* she in?"

Upstairs in the VIP suite, Jeremy had quickly figured out exactly how to keep the beautiful girl in the bed entranced. All he'd had to do, when she asked him about himself, was pretend to be his father as he imagined Thomas Barlow might have been when he was studying to become a cardiologist. His father had talked about it often enough. When he wasn't boring everyone with how successful and powerful he was now, he was talking about how hard it had been to get there. How long the hours were, how little sleep, how little money. Hard to believe his father had ever been poor, but he had.

Those were the stories Jeremy drew on to create for Amber the picture of a struggling young intern. "I'm always broke," he concluded, leaning back in his chair the way his father did. Too bad he didn't have a pipe. That would have helped. "But one day," he said with feigned assurance, "I expect to be Chief Cardiologist of this medical complex. Maybe I'll buy a . . . a Rolls-Royce." His father drove a Cadillac, but it didn't hurt to change the details a little. "And a mansion on Linden Hill."

Amber's eyes brightened considerably at the mention of a mansion. This boy certainly was cute. Too bad he wasn't just a tiny bit taller. If they went out, would she be able to wear heels? She couldn't tell, with him seated. She'd have to wait until he stood up to be sure. She *had* to wear heels.

He looked awfully young to be an intern, which probably meant that he was really smart and had skipped a grade or two. Chief Cardiologist. That had a nice ring to it. Doctor and Mrs. Jeremy Noone? Not bad. *Only*, of course, if Leo had the gall to replace her. As long as she had her career, marriage wasn't a consideration.

But if the career went down the tubes, sickening thought, she might *need* this cute, smart boy. He probably had lots of women hanging around him, though, if he was going to be a doctor. She'd better pull out all the stops, just in case.

"Could you get me a fresh pitcher of water?" she asked, trying to make herself sound as helpless as possible. *Helpless* wasn't ordinarily a word in her vocabulary, and everyone she worked with would have been hysterical with laughter at the idea. But she *was* an actress, after all. Playing helpless wasn't such a major challenge. She'd had harder jobs. "I'm so thirsty. The air in here is so dry, don't you think?"

Jeremy practically fell over himself in his rush to do her bidding. When he had disappeared inside the bathroom with Amber's pitcher, she yanked open her nightstand drawer and grabbed her perfume, lip gloss, and a hairbrush. She dabbed a few drops of perfume behind her ears and on her wrists, applied a dab of lip gloss, and ran the brush through her hair before tossing everything back into the drawer. No point in looking *too* sick.

When Jeremy returned with the refilled pitcher and set it on the tray table, Amber beamed her most potent smile up at him and said sweetly, "Oh, thank you so much, Dr. Noone! This is so sweet of you. How can I ever thank you?"

They had only been talking for another three or four minutes when the lovely face suddenly turned scarlet. The beautiful blue eyes widened, and the delicate hands flew to her swanlike throat.

With great difficulty, Amber's head turned on the pillow, toward the boy she thought of as "Dr. Noone." "I can't breathe!" she gasped. "I can't breathe! Help me! Do something!"

chapter
10

Jeremy panicked. Amber, clutching her throat and gasping that she couldn't breathe, was looking to *him* for help. She thought he was an intern . . . because he had *told* her he was. She thought he would know what to do in a medical emergency, which this clearly *was*. His stupid plan to impress her was blowing up in his face.

Because he couldn't think of anything else to do, he grabbed the buzzer lying beside her and pressed it fiercely, then punched it again and again when no one responded.

No one responded because Amber had cried wolf too many times. A nurse at the desk, busy preparing a medication tray, noticed the signal from the VIP suite, and shook her head. "What now?" she murmured under her breath. "More ice cubes? Not enough channels on the TV? The fire sirens are disturbing her rest? I'm busy." She placed another tiny paper cup holding two white capsules on the tray. "It's not like this is Intensive Care. The only thing wrong with our friend in there is a bad case of third-degree arrogance.

She can just wait until I'm done here."

Amber's face and throat were an angry scarlet. In her futile struggle to breathe, her long, pointed fingernails dug into her throat. Jeremy could see the deep scratches her scarlet nails were gouging into her skin. Her mouth was wide open in an effort to gulp air into her lungs, but she no longer made any sound. Her eyes began to roll back in her head.

Jeremy dropped the buzzer and bolted, racing to the door to shout for help. "Somebody get in here," he shouted wildly. "Something is really wrong! Hurry!"

There was no mistaking the urgency in his voice. The nurse at the desk dropped the medication tray and ran in rubber-soled shoes to the suite. A second nurse in a room across the hall heard Jeremy's cry for help, and hurried to see what the problem was.

"Pulse one-forty and barely palpable," the first nurse said when she had lifted one of Amber's wrists. "Breathing rapid and shallow." She called to Jeremy over her shoulder, "What happened here?"

"I don't know. We were talking and then she just got like this, all of a sudden."

The nurse hastily wrapped a blood pressure cuff around Amber's upper arm and pumped it up. "Did you have an argument? Was she upset?"

Her tone of voice seemed accusatory to Jeremy, and his own tone became defensive. "No! Like I said, we were just talking. It happened so fast. What's wrong with her?"

The nurse didn't answer him. "BP ninety over sixty. Get someone in here *now*!" she ordered the second nurse. "This girl is in acute respiratory distress. We need an airway, stat, or we're going to lose her."

Jeremy stared at her. *Lose* her? What was the nurse talking about?

Moments after the second nurse ran from the room, she returned with a young doctor Jeremy didn't recognize. One glance at the semiconscious girl in the bed led to an order for an IV, which the first nurse had already begun to set up, and an immediate dosage of a drug called epinephrine. Jeremy thought it was used in heart cases, but he wasn't sure. Something was wrong with Amber's heart? Was that why she'd come to Emsee? When he'd asked her why she was in the hospital, she had shrugged and said, "Who knows? No one seems to."

But then the doctor said, "Looks like anaphylaxis." He was listening to Amber's chest sounds with his stethoscope. "What was she eating? Did you bring her food?" he demanded of Jeremy.

"Food?" Jeremy was stunned. Another accusation. As if he'd done something wrong. And he hadn't. Well, he *had*, he'd lied to Amber, but *they* didn't know that. "No, I didn't bring her any food. I just *met* her."

The doctor's sharp gaze spied the white Styrofoam container in the wastebasket under Amber's bed. "Like hell you didn't. The evidence is right there. What was in that thing?"

"I don't *know!*" With three pairs of accusing eyes on him, Jeremy felt trapped. He was wishing he had never stepped inside this hospital room, no matter how pretty the girl in the bed was. "I didn't bring her anything to eat."

The doctor persisted. "This looks like it could be an MSG reaction."

Jeremy knew what MSG was. Monosodium glutamate, a chemical commonly added to food. He also knew it could cause allergic reactions in some people. He knew that because those patients were sometimes mistakenly diagnosed as heart attack victims, so his father was often called in to help. He came home after those incidents ranting and raving about having to waste his precious time on "false alarms."

"Well, whatever it is," Jeremy said angrily, "I didn't bring it in here. Someone else must have."

As if on cue, Amber's manager and agent appeared in the doorway. "What on earth . . . ?" the woman cried when she saw the activity around the bed and the patient thrashing among the bed linens trying in vain to catch her breath. "What's wrong?"

One of the nurses hurried to gently lead the pair back out into the hall. "She's very sick," she explained, "and you'll only get in the way. Please wait out here. We're doing everything we can." She hesitated, then asked, "Has this happened to her before?"

"Oh, not like *this*," Bess answered, her anxious eyes on the doorway to Amber's room. "She's had some difficulty breathing from time to time. The doctors in New York think it's emotional, the result of stress. Panic attacks, they called it. Stress comes with the territory in our business. But I've never seen her this bad. Can't you *do* something?"

"We're doing the best we can."

The nurse had just turned and re-entered the room when Susannah and Callie emerged from the elevator. Astrid hadn't relented and revealed any information about the new patient, but Callie knew the hospital well, and she wasn't stupid. "She's in the VIP suite, isn't she?" she had demanded, adding, "and you can't keep me away from there, so don't even try."

All Astrid could do was send Susannah along with Callie, saying, "Try to keep her out of everyone's hair if you can, okay?"

Kate had refused to accompany the two girls,

saying she wasn't the least bit interested in an autograph from someone who had been complaining her head off ever since she walked through Emsee's doors. The truth was, she didn't want to leave the desk in case Damon called in with information about the fire. It was the *fire* she was interested in, but it wouldn't be such a bad thing to know that *he* was okay, too. After all, he'd once been a friend. Kate Thompson cared about her friends. You could ask anyone, they'd tell you that was true. Susannah didn't want to leave, either. She still hadn't heard anything further about Abby's father. Her stomach felt like it was tied in a knot. But Astrid was firm about Callie being accompanied upstairs, so Susannah gave in.

"Uh-oh," she said when she saw the agent and manager pacing anxiously outside the suite, "something's going on. You might have to forget about that autograph, Callie."

Undeterred, Callie strode purposefully toward the agent. "Excuse me," she said when she was standing in front of the woman, "I'm Callie Matthews. My father runs this entire medical complex. I need to see Amber Taylor."

As Susannah joined them, she heard from inside the room, "Blood pressure still falling. Seventy over fifty. Pulse one-fifty, respiration thirty-six and labored. The epi isn't doing the trick."

"Then hit her again, oh-three megs of epi,

stat. Continue the oxygen. And make sure that drip's open all the way."

The group in the hall listened.

"Blood pressure still falling!"

"What's wrong?" Callie asked the agent.

The woman ignored her, moving closer to the doorway to watch the harried activity inside. Susannah did the same. When she spotted Jeremy, standing back against the wall, his face pale, his eyes on the bed, she cleared her throat to get his attention, then summoned him with a crook of her finger. He seemed relieved to leave the room.

"What's going on?" she asked when he joined them. "What were you doing in there? And what's wrong with that girl?"

"I guess it's an allergic reaction," he answered, turning back to watch from the doorway. "She can't breathe. And her face is really red. She keeps clawing at her throat, like she's choking. The doctor's going to put something down her throat to let her breathe. Some kind of tube. They act like it's my fault, but I didn't do anything. We were talking and she was fine, and then all of a sudden, she wasn't."

Callie looked envious. "You were actually *talking* to Amber Taylor? How'd you manage that?"

Jeremy's answer was drowned out by the doctor's voice calling for a dopamine drip. Susannah thought that meant the epinephrine still wasn't working.

"We need blood gases, portable chest X ray, and an EKG," the doctor commanded. "Move it, people, this girl's in distress! I want a Benadryl drip. And monitor her heart rate. Let me know the minute her blood pressure goes above ninety systolic."

The activity at Amber's bedside continued at a furious rate. To Susannah, watching from the hall, the patient seemed to have needles and tubes in her everywhere. Then they had to move out of the way as various staff members carrying equipment arrived and hurried into the room. The portable chest X-ray machine arrived, then an EKG machine. Its small rubber suction cups were attached to the patient's chest to monitor her heart rate. A nurse continued to call out pulse, respiration, and blood pressure at regular intervals.

Susannah listened anxiously for the news that Amber's blood pressure had gone above ninety, which would mean that she was responding to the medication dripping steadily into her veins.

"I don't understand," Amber's agent murmured as she paced back and forth on the white tile in the hallway. "She's never had an attack this serious before. And she was fine when we left to go eat. She said she was going to nap."

"The doctor accused me of giving her the wrong thing to eat," Jeremy said. "But I didn't. I didn't give her *anything*."

The manager overheard. His head shot up. "They think it's something she ate?" He flashed a guilty glance toward the agent. "Jeez, you think it coulda been the lunch we brought her? Think they put something in that Caesar salad that could do this to her?"

"You brought her food?" Susannah asked.

The agent nodded. "Was that the wrong thing to do? She insisted she was starving, and I didn't see how it could hurt."

The woman looked so guilt-stricken, Susannah made her voice gentle. "She might be on a special diet, especially if she's scheduled for any blood work. It's probably not a good idea to give her food that isn't on her hospital menu, at least for now."

"It's kind of like not feeding the animals at the zoo," Callie added dryly, smiling sweetly at Amber's friends. She wanted the two of them to like her. They were obviously in charge of the actress, and if she was nice to them now when they were so worried, maybe later they'd let her in to see the patient. When this crisis was over, of course. "Only there aren't any signs posted here like there are at the zoo, so you couldn't have known. It's not your fault." It would be great fun to go back to school on Monday and tell everyone she'd spent part of her weekend with "Lynette." Wouldn't the other girls just tear their hair out with jealousy? She could hardly wait.

"I have to get back downstairs," Susannah reluctantly told Callie and Jeremy. She hated to leave. She knew from her classes that anaphylactic shock could be life-threatening, and clearly was in this case. Susannah had no trouble imagining how terrifying the sudden inability to breathe could be. Patients in that condition, whatever the reason for it, always panicked, which just made things worse. "There's still a fire out there," Susannah added, "so I might be needed in Emergency." She didn't mention how worried she was about Abby's father. And about Will. To Jeremy, she said, "Stop down in ER before you leave the building, okay, and let me know how this turns out?"

He nodded absentmindedly, his eyes still focused on the figure, no longer thrashing but lying quietly now.

But Susannah didn't have to wait for Jeremy to come to her later with news of Amber. Just before she stepped into the elevator, she saw the doctor emerge from the suite and approach the agent and the manager. And she could tell by the demeanor of all three that the worst had been averted. They talked quietly, calmly, with no outward signs of shock, and the agent seemed to sag slightly in relief. Then nurses and orderlies began leaving the room, carrying equipment. The epi and the dopamine drip had finally taken hold. The girl must be breathing on her own again, or that equipment would be staying in the suite.

Susannah was surprised by the intensity of her own relief. She didn't even know the actress. Had never heard of her, and wasn't a fan, like Callie and her friends. All she knew so far was that Amber Taylor was young, and pretty spoiled. But being spoiled didn't mean you deserved to be sick, or to come that close to dying.

Maybe, Susannah thought as she stepped into the elevator, maybe since the staff pulled her back from the edge, she'll appreciate Emsee more, and stop complaining so much.

Then she remembered the fuss over the flat-heeled slippers and thought, well, maybe not.

chapter
11

At the refinery, Abby clutched her mother's hand tightly. They stood together, leaning against the ambulance, facing the burning structure. The heat and the flames had lessened somewhat as firemen continued to level hoses on the building. Never taking their eyes away from what was left of the entrance, watching desperately for some sign of Brendan O'Connor, mother and daughter were unaware that the blaze had moved on.

Whipped by the vicious wind, the flames had galloped at breakneck speed from tree to tree until there was a solid canopy of fire above and behind all of the buildings marching up the site. The blaze, now a giant, heated vacuum intent on swallowing up everything in its path, consumed limb and leaf and branch and trunk. At the same time, a separate, thick snake of fire sped along the ground below, headed straight for the nearest cluster of oil tanks. A group of yellow-slickered firemen had left the building, intent on heading off the snake before it reached its incendiary target.

"God, I feel so helpless," Sid complained to Sam. They had stayed where they were, in the shadows of the warehouse, not wanting to get in the way when Abby and her mother moved to the ambulance. "Abby's a wreck, and there's nothing I can say or do to make her feel better. If I wasn't in this stupid wheelchair . . ."

"Explain that connection to me," Sam said calmly. "What's your chair got to do with anything? Are you saying that if you could walk, you'd run into that burning building to rescue your girlfriend's father? Now there's a smart move. *I* have full use of my lower extremities, but you don't see me rushing into that inferno, do you? That's because I'm not stupid. Think about it. Anyway, the firemen would never let either one of us get that close. It's *their* job to get people out of there, Costello. That's what they *do*. You're no fireman."

"I'm no *anything*," Sid retorted with a bitterness that would have surprised Abby. She was convinced that Sid had moved beyond that. And to some extent, he had, thanks in part to her upbeat, stubborn insistence that he *could* get better. But the helplessness that he was feeling as he watched her suffering brought back all of the bitterness in a chilling wave. One day, last summer, he had been like Sam, a strong, healthy athlete. Then he had fallen from Grant's water tower during a stupid, juvenile prank, and the next day he couldn't feel his own legs. Hadn't felt them since. "Yeah," he told Sam emphatically, "I *would* go in there if I thought I could find Abby's dad and bring him out."

"Well, that's real smart, Sid." Sam's voice was matter-of-fact. "I guess you must have hit your head when you dove off that water tower. You don't know any more about fighting fires than you do about how much a girl expects from a guy. You think that would make Abby happy, seeing her boyfriend run into a burning building? No way. Look, if O'Connor's father is in there, the firemen will find him and bring him out."

Sid shook his head. His eyes were watering from the thick smoke, and his throat felt raw. He was a good distance away from the fire. How much worse must it be *inside* that building? "You really think there's any chance at all that someone inside could still be alive?" Abby talked about her father a lot, with the kind of warmth and admiration that Sid hoped she would someday use when she talked about *him*. What would it do to her if something happened to her father? She would never be the same again.

"Sure, there's a good chance," Sam said heartily. "O'Connor was in Vietnam. Probably knows a thing or two about survival. Maybe he found a little cubbyhole to hide in, away from the smoke and fire. Stranger things have happened."

Sid didn't think Sam sounded all that convinced. He was probably just saying what he thought Sid needed to hear.

Two more fire trucks roared onto the scene, then a third. One parked between the burning structure and the warehouse, blocking Sid's view of the fire scene.

So he wasn't able to see the coughing, choking fireman who staggered into the doorway half-dragging, half-carrying a limp figure whose face and hair and once-white shirt and tan pants were black with smoke.

But Abby and her mother saw the figures.

"Oh, God," Abby whispered, taking a step forward. "Mom?"

The fireman, one arm still clutching his burden, collapsed in the doorway.

Will and two other paramedics rushed to his aid. "Get a stretcher!" Will shouted as he knelt, one hand over his mouth against the smoke. "The other guy's unconscious."

Two firemen came to help. In seconds, both victims were safely away from the building. The fireman who had performed the rescue was still able to walk. He was helped to the ambulance, propped between two members of his team, while Will and his partner hurried to the ambulance with the stretcher. They immediately began administering oxygen to both men.

Charlie O'Connor, still gripping her daughter's hand, dashed forward to intercept the stretcher. "Brendan? Is that Brendan?" She stared down at the face partially hidden beneath the oxygen mask and streaked with charcoal. "Oh, God, I can't *tell!* She reached out then, hesitantly, to lift the limp left hand. Her index finger ran along the ring finger. She gasped when she felt the heat of the gold band, but she persisted, fingering the ring silently. Then she nodded, saying in a near-whisper, "It's him. This is his ring." Her eyes went to Will. "Is he dead? *Is* he?"

Will shook his head. He had never in his life been so glad to answer, "No. No, he's not dead."

Brendan O'Connor's wife sagged against her daughter. "He's not dead!"

"We've got to get him to the hospital. You can ride in the back with him, Mrs. O'Connor. Abby, I'm sorry, but there's no room up front. Sam will have to bring you."

Abby whirled and ran.

Throughout the harrowing trip to the hospital in Sam's van, Sid gripped Abby's hand in his and murmured reassuring words. He knew she wasn't hearing him. But he couldn't stand the agonized look on her face, couldn't sit by silently while she was in such pain. So he said things like, "It's probably not as bad as it looks," and, "Your dad's strong and healthy, right? He can beat this," and, "Will's a great paramedic, he knows what he's doing, he'll take good care of your dad," knowing as the words spilled out of him that they were falling on deaf ears.

He was right. Abby, sitting rigid with fear beside him, was lost in a terrifying world where the only image she could see was her father's form lying on that stretcher, his clothing singed, his face black with smoke. She tried in vain to tell herself all the things that Sid, unheard, was telling her: It couldn't be that bad, it just couldn't, because what would they do if it was? How could they ever go home and tell Geneva, Moira, Carmel, and Mattie their father wasn't coming home? And Toothless, the baby, not yet three, would be lost without her daddy.

The sickening image of her big, strong father lying unconscious on that stretcher stuck to her mind like ugly graffiti.

At Med Center, news of incoming traffic had sent Kate and Susannah, along with other staff members, outside to await the ambulance. The rampaging wind tore at their hair and smocks, and the acrid smell of smoke stung their eyes. An air of anxiety settled over the group as they gathered under Emergency's rear canopy.

Prior to the call for help, Kate and Susannah had been discussing the frightening episode in the VIP suite. Susannah had filled Kate in on the details. Now Kate resumed the conversation over the distant wail of the approaching ambulance by saying, "If you ask me, the only thing Emsee's newest celebrity is allergic to is not getting her own way. Someone probably told her we don't provide room service, and the news sent her into anaphylactic shock."

"Kate, that's not funny." Susannah swiped at her stinging eyes with a tissue. The sun that had been shining earlier, turning the autumn leaves to stained-glass colors, was now well-hidden behind the thick curtain of black smoke overhead. "She could have died."

Kate's hands went to her hips, and her voice became indignant. "Are you implying that Emsee can't handle a simple allergic reaction?"

The approaching siren grew louder. Susannah had to raise her voice to be heard. "I'm not implying any such thing. Of course we can. All I'm saying is that she really came close to dying. Whatever it was she ate, it almost killed her."

"Probably caviar she had flown in from Russia," Kate muttered unforgivingly.

Then the ambulance arrived, screeching to a halt at the entrance, and the flurry of activity began.

Will was the first person to jump from the ambulance. Susannah couldn't see the face of the patient lifted out on the first stretcher and gently but swiftly placed on a waiting gurney. But she could tell by the scorched scalp above the oxygen mask and the angry red areas of skin below the cuff of the sleeves that this was not simply a case of smoke inhalation. Worse than the red were the dirty-gray areas on the ankles and wrists. The red might only be first- or second-degree burns, but the skin that looked like wrinkled, dirty white tissue paper was probably third-degree, the worst burn.

Susannah realized that what she was looking at was the refinery fire's first burn victim.

She ran to hold the ER door open.

When Will passed with the gurney and saw her standing there, he said brusquely, almost apologetically, "It's Abby's dad."

Susannah gasped, "Oh, no!" She would never have recognized him. At almost the same moment, Charlie O'Connor exited the ambulance, and Sam's silver van careened up the driveway, stopping short with an agonizing squeal of brakes. Abby flew out of the car before it had come to a complete halt and ran after her mother. The two brushed past Susannah in the wake of the gurney, their faces strained and pale.

Too shocked to think clearly, Susannah managed only, "Oh, God, Abby, I'm sorry!"

Abby, intent on catching up with the gurney, didn't hear.

Sam yanked Sid's chair out of the van and

helped him into it. "How is she?" Susannah asked Sid as they passed. Mute, he shook his head, and they went on inside.

Remembering that the call had stated *two* incoming patients, Susannah stayed where she was. She would get to Abby as soon as she could.

The second figure lifted from the ambulance was also masked with the plastic cup feeding him oxygen, but he was wearing the yellow slicker of a fireman. He was helmetless.

The minute Kate saw the thick, dark, curly hair, she knew it was Damon. A "hot dog," Will had told her, and here was the proof. He'd gone into that burning building, probably alone, to drag O'Connor's father free. She knew it without being told. And she couldn't decide whether that made Damon Lawrence brave, or just plain stupid.

He was conscious, and murmuring words Kate couldn't decipher. Something about a wall collapsing, she thought. One pant leg was badly burned, and, she guessed, probably the leg itself, although Damon wouldn't be feeling the pain yet.

"Must have taken off his mask while he was inside," a paramedic named John told Kate as they began wheeling the gurney inside. "He probably gave it to the guy he rescued. Looks to me like he's swallowed a whole bunch of smoke."

The fireman reached up to lift the oxygen mask away from his face. "Had to," he gasped. "Had to take . . . off . . . mask. Call . . . the guy's

. . . name. O'Connor. See if he'd answer me . . . so I could find him."

Kate's hand shot out to clamp the plastic cup firmly in place again. "Shut up!" she commanded. "Just shut up and breathe."

Damon subsided obediently.

When they had taken his gurney into a trauma room, Susannah left to find Abby. Abby and her mother were sitting, white-faced and huddled together, on a blue plastic-covered bench in the ER waiting room.

"Can I get you something?" Susannah asked quietly, eager to do something, *anything*, to help.

Abby lifted her head. "Just go see how he is, okay? You can do that. You can find out. Please."

Susannah nodded. She hurried off to find Brendan O'Connor's trauma room. Unless he hadn't been as seriously burned as it looked, he'd be whisked over to the burn unit as soon as possible. But he'd receive his emergency care here first.

She found him amid a bustle of activity in trauma room A. He was still unconscious, and receiving oxygen. His scorched clothing had been cut away and an IV inserted in his left arm. Instead of Jonah Izbecki, the doctor in charge was Dr. Lincoln, a tall, attractive brunette Susannah had worked with many times. Lincoln specialized in burn cases, and Susannah was relieved that she'd been called in.

The nurse covered Abby's father with two sterile sheets and doused them with saline solution. She was dispensing the second quart when Dr. Lincoln began speaking rapidly. "Call respiratory for intubation. We need an airway here. Then call the lab. And I want a chest X ray and an EKG, per usual, because while it looks bad, I think our big problem here is still smoke, not fire. We've got about a twenty-five percent burn case here. I've seen worse."

Susannah breathed a sigh of relief. They used something called the Rule of Nines in calculating the percentage of a victim's body that had suffered severe burns. Brendan O'Connor's, surprisingly, was twenty-five percent, not a high figure considering that he'd been trapped for so long. She had seen cases that were much higher, as high as seventy-five percent. But those patients hadn't lived.

She could go back to Abby and tell her that at least the burn damage, while painful, wasn't threatening her father's life. But she couldn't be as optimistic about the smoke inhalation.

"Most of the serious burn damage," Dr. Lincoln concluded, "is to the back. Although he seems to have landed on his face when he fell, judging by this ugly bruise on his forehead, he must have rolled over onto his back. He'll be lying on his stomach while he recuperates." But then she bent to listen to his chest again. When she straightened up, she was frowning. "I don't like the sound of this. *Where* is respiratory?"

Susannah's anxiety intensified. Maybe it wasn't going to matter that he hadn't been severely burned.

The respiratory technician hurried into the room to quickly set up suction and prepared the instruments for inserting a tube into the patient's lungs to help him breathe.

"Mr. O'Connor?" Dr. Lincoln said softly, although there was no sign from the patient that he was hearing her. "I'm going to very carefully put this tube down your nose into your lungs so that you can breathe properly. But first, I'm going to give you a mild sedative so the insertion of the tube won't be too painful. Just hang in there with me, okay? We'll be finished in just a sec."

Abby's father stirred and groaned.

When he had been minimally sedated and the breathing tube inserted, he was carefully rolled over onto his stomach, his burns were wrapped in sterile gauze strips soaked in saline, and blankets were spread over him to conserve whatever body heat he might have been generating.

While he was being prepared for transport to the burn unit, Dr. Lincoln left the room to explain to the patient's family what his condition was and what his chances were.

Susannah went with her.

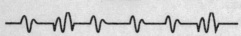

In trauma room C, Kate stood beside the table where Damon lay, receiving pure oxygen by mask. Nurses hurriedly cut his yellow slicker away from his body so that Dr. Izbecki could assess his burns. Damon was conscious. His eyes above the mask were raw and red, his high, angled cheekbones scarlet. A blister was already appearing on his lower lip.

Kate was torn. She wasn't sure if she wanted to hold his hand or give it a sharp crack with a sturdy ruler. One of the firemen had told her that Damon had gone into the burning building alone, looking for Abby's father. Idiot, idiot! How could he have been so reckless? She was certain they weren't taught to behave so carelessly during the firefighter course. As usual, Damon was making up his own rules as he went along.

Dr. Izbecki listened carefully to Damon's chest, while a nurse removed the patient's boots and thick socks. When she pulled the second boot off, a layer of skin came with it, soft and crumpled like tissue paper, as if the nurse were unwrapping a gift. Kate winced, but Damon didn't seem to feel it.

The chest X ray showed no serious lung damage, and his only burn other than the one on his leg was the searing of his facial skin, which was treated with ointment and sterile cloths.

While Dr. Izbecki conferred with the nurses about whether or not to send Damon to the burn unit, Kate leaned over the table, putting her mouth close to his ear. "So," she whispered angrily, "you just had to be a hero, didn't you? I guess you miss all that applause you used to get on the football field, right? Well, guess again, Fireman Lawrence. Going into that building alone was just stupid, and no one's applauding."

He reached up to push the mask to one side. A spasm of coughing stopped him from speaking, but when it had passed, he grinned up at her. "Yeah, they are," he said hoarsely. "I bet that girl and her mother are clapping their hands plenty. Man, were they glad to see me pull that guy outa there! Maybe if you'd been there, and seen their faces, you'd have a little respect for your old pal."

He was maddening. "A burning building isn't anything like a football field," Kate snapped, straightening up and pushing the oxygen mask back into place.

He pushed it aside again. "You got that right. A football field's a whole lot more dangerous," he joked, and then another coughing spasm forced him to replace the mask.

It was decided not to send him to the burn unit. His leg was treated and bandaged and he was admitted to a room on the fourth floor.

Kate was first surprised, then annoyed, by the way the news made her feel. Realizing that she was *glad* he wasn't being transferred to Miller set her teeth on edge. She didn't want to be glad. She didn't want to care one way or the other.

"Come up and see me," he called as he was wheeled to the elevator. "I hate hospital rooms!"

"Then you shouldn't have risked your neck!" she retorted. But she saw the way people in the waiting room fixed their eyes on his gurney and began nodding and talking among themselves, and she knew what they were saying. Damon Lawrence was a hero. Just as he had been on the football field. Abby's father was very popular, so a lot of people would be grateful to the person who had saved him. Everyone in town would be talking about Brendan O'Connor's rescue. Damon would be on the news tonight.

Shaking her head, Kate went to the waiting room to see who was next in line for treatment.

But she was also wondering how soon she could take her break. Maybe she'd stop in and see Damon. Just to make sure he had everything he needed. She *was* a volunteer, after all. It was part of her job to see that patients had what they needed.

"You're being awfully rough on him," Susannah said later when they were collecting more rolls of sterile gauze in one of the supply rooms. The conversation had turned to the rescue. "I mean, he *did* save Abby's father's life, Kate. He could have died doing it. I thought you admired bravery. You thought Jeremy was pretty special for rescuing you from the library roof the night of the flood. Why are you so down on this guy Damon? Don't you like him?"

Then, although Kate said nothing, something must have shown in her face. Because when Susannah glanced over to see why Kate hadn't answered her, suspicion appeared in her bright blue eyes. "Hey, what's this?" Enlightenment quickly replaced the suspicion. "It's not that you don't like him, is it? It's just the opposite. You *do* like him, and that makes you mad, right, Kate? You're afraid he'll get in your way. Come on, Kate, give him a chance. If he turns out to be a jerk," she added dryly, "you can always send him into another burning building."

"I've known Damon Lawrence since we were eight, and I already *know* he's a jerk." Her arms filled with supplies, Kate turned to leave. "And I'd appreciate it if you wouldn't start handing out advice. Especially," she added caustically, "since you haven't done such a great job of managing your own love life." She made a great show of glancing around the spacious closet. "I don't see Will Jackson around here anywhere, do you?"

"Okay, be that way." Susannah felt her cheeks growing warm. "Just don't blame me when you're a lonely old lady, practicing medicine during the day and going home to your cat at night."

Kate relaxed then, laughing as she turned out the light. "Maybe we could be lonely old ladies together, okay? But no cats. I'm allergic. It's a dog or nothing."

"Okay, a dog it is. But I get to name it."

"Done."

The fire continued to rage out of control, consuming in short order a park where Eastridge children played, seven houses behind the park, and an abandoned railway before it began to gobble up a small white church. Three more firemen were brought to Emsee in ambulances. Only one was able to return to the fire.

At the burn unit, Sid sat with Sam in the waiting room while Abby and her mother conferred with the specialists who would be treating Brendan O'Connor. As they waited, they watched live coverage of the fire scene. Following the coverage came a plea for volunteers to hose down houses in the area.

"I should go on over there," Sam said. "Can't sit by and let the whole city burn down around us, right?"

"If you go, I'm going, too. I can aim a hose at a house."

Someone else might have said, "Are you kidding? A fire is no place for a wheelchair." Or, more kindly, "No, Abby needs you here." But Sam's school had played Sid's in football. And lost. Sam knew better than most people that Sid Costello was made of strong stuff. So all he said was, "Yeah, sure. Come on, then. You want to tell O'Connor we're out of here?"

Sid debated. He was afraid Abby would say the things that Sam hadn't. They'd been getting along really well since he'd started making an effort to get better. The truth was, he was crazy about her. And the way she looked at him sometimes, usually just before he kissed her, made him feel he could do anything. But she was upset now, about her father, and might not react the way she normally would. If she even hinted that he would be useless at a fire scene, he wasn't sure he could forgive her.

"Nah," he said far more casually than he felt. "She's busy. She's got more important things on her mind than the comings and goings of Sid Costello. Let's just go, okay? I need to feel useful."

Abby did turn, just once, and glance in their direction as they turned to leave. But she was so caught up in the treatment the doctors were describing, and thinking how painful it was going to be for her father, that their departure didn't really register. If she wondered where they were going, the question remained unasked as she turned back to her mother.

Callie Matthews was sitting in a straight-backed chair in the hallway outside the VIP suite when Jeremy stepped off the elevator, his arms filled with one dozen yellow long-stemmed roses purchased in the gift shop behind the lobby downstairs.

"Wow!" Callie stood up, tossing her long, blonde hair. "Not trying to impress somebody, are you?" Jealous that Jeremy had actually spent time with Amber Taylor, she added disdainfully, "She probably gets those all the time, from all her admirers in New York."

Jeremy had known Callie for a long time, and her comments never bothered him very much. "Maybe. But these are from *me*. And her admirers aren't *here*, are they?"

"They won't let you see her," she said confidently. "Those people who brought her in here are still too shook up over her allergy attack. You'll never get inside."

Jeremy strode forward and knocked on the closed door.

It was opened by the agent. "Yes?"

"I'm Jeremy. I was here before." He held out the bouquet. "I brought these for her."

"That's him!" a voice called weakly from the bed. "That's the one I told you about. Dr. Noone. He helped me. Let him in."

The door was pulled open wide and Jeremy entered the suite.

The door closed.

Outside, in the hallway, Callie fumed. And thought, *Dr.* Noone? Who's he kidding?

Callie wasted no time deciding how to best put to use what she had just overheard.

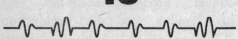

It took a lot to shock Sam Grant, to ruffle his cool. But when he and Sid arrived in Eastridge and saw the devastation wrought by the fire, he was visibly shaken. Residents who had left that morning for work or errands or shopping had returned at the sound of the refinery siren to watch as their homes went up in flames. East Sixty-third Street was crowded with area residents milling about, their faces gray with smoke, their eyes bewildered. Because the fire had already had its fill of their block and raced onward, most of the firemen had left, chasing the flames. Only a few had remained behind to keep an eye on dangerous "hot spots" and make sure the fire really was finished with this street.

Off in the distance, Sam and Sid could see the scarlet flames continuing to swallow up the woods and the refinery site and Eastridge itself. But where they were standing, they were surrounded by the wet, blackened wrecks of homes. They stood in puddles of water and foam the firemen had left behind.

"We tried to hose it down," a young woman with two small children at her side told a shaken Sam as he reached the street corner where she was standing. Her eyes never left the smoldering pile of rubble on the opposite corner. "But the water pressure here in Eastridge stinks. We couldn't get much more than a trickle. It just wasn't enough." She looked up at him with tear-swollen eyes, and then, with no apparent curiosity, at Sid in his wheelchair. "All we have left," she said, "is what's on our backs. That's it. Even my old Chevy's gone." She laughed bitterly. "I thought it'd be nice if me and the kids walked to the school. My oldest was singing in a concert there. I wouldn't have missed it for the world. The car wasn't much, I guess, but it got me to work and back. I don't know how I'll get to work now." She laughed again, and fresh tears filled her eyes. "What's the matter with me? My *house* is gone! I don't even know where I'll be living, so how do I even know I'll *need* a car to get to work?"

Sam realized she wasn't really talking to them, and didn't expect a response. Not that he had one to give. What did you say to someone who'd just lost everything? Well, not quite everything. They were alive.

Taking her children by the hand, the woman walked across the street to get a better look at the smoldering wreckage of her home. Two neighbors tried to stop her, but she kept going.

"Nothing we can do here," Sid said when his dark eyes had surveyed the damage. Sickened, he stared at the burned-out shells of houses, the weeping neighbors comforting one another, the blackened trees and shrubs and fences and flower beds, still sending out plumes of smoke. "We'd better try another block, one the fire hasn't touched yet. Maybe we can actually save someone's house if we wet it down enough."

"We need more than just the two of us. I'm going to hike back to the van and use my phone to call out the troops." Sid knew Sam was referring to his many friends, most of them athletes with strength and boundless energy. "They're probably just sitting around watching the fire on television, anyway. Might as well get their butts over here and see the real thing, right? I'll be right back."

While he waited, Sid thought of Abby. Was she wondering where he was? Probably not. The only thing she'd have on her mind right now was her father. What was the name of that fireman who had pulled O'Connor out of the building? Lawrence. The same Lawrence who'd raced across the football field when Sid was a sophomore? Man, that guy had been fast! The newspapers had called him "Lightning Lawrence." He'd been a cinch for All-State. Then he'd just disappeared. Someone said he'd dropped out. Dumb move for him, but helpful to Sid, who'd made All-State instead.

I wasn't half as fast as he was, though, Sid thought honestly. Never would have been, either, even if I hadn't fallen off that stupid water tower.

Sam returned, saying "the guys" would meet them on East Sixty-first Street, if the firemen would let them through.

"They'll let them through," Sid vowed. "They called for volunteers, didn't they?"

"Yeah, but only for parts of the city that aren't already burning," Sam said as they started out, walking in the middle of the street away from the smoking embers, like everyone else. "We can't go into any area that's burning. It's too dangerous. We're not here to fight the fire, we're here to try to save some homes." He reached out to deliver a warning tap to Sid's shoulder. "So no heroics, promise?"

"Like I have a choice. Some hero I'd make."

Sam's friends were waiting when they reached Sixty-first Street. Although a thick wall of flame was approaching rapidly from the direction of the refinery, the homes there were still untouched by fire. Directed by the firemen, all of the boys grabbed up garden hoses and began watering down roofs and siding.

Amber Taylor's agent and manager left their charge alone with Jeremy. He had been introduced to them as "Dr. Noone." Since Amber had embroidered Jeremy's role in saving her life, they believed she was safe in his hands, and went downstairs to have coffee.

"I really didn't do that much," Jeremy pointed out when they had gone and he'd taken a seat beside the patient's bed. "That kind of allergy attack isn't exactly my specialty. I don't know that much about it . . . yet." He felt bad, lying to her when she'd been through such a bad time. But he was too embarrassed to tell her the truth now. Anyway, it probably wouldn't be good for her now, when she was so weak from the attack. He should wait until she was stronger.

Her face was still slightly flushed, and she looked as beautiful to him as ever. She reached out and patted his hand. "You knew enough to get help. You saved my life." Her lower lip came out in a pout. "I know those nurses wouldn't have answered the buzzer if you hadn't yelled at them. They hate me. Just because I'm famous, they think I'm a spoiled brat." She smiled at Jeremy, leaving her hand carelessly on top of his. "*You* don't think I'm spoiled, do you?" Before he could answer, she added harshly, "If they only knew how hard it was to get where I am!" Then she sank back against the pillow and said so quietly that Jeremy really didn't catch the words, "And how afraid I am of losing it all. . . ."

Jeremy didn't tell her he had never heard of

her. He was afraid it would upset her. He was also afraid she would ask him to tell her what it was like being a doctor. To avoid that, he quickly asked her what it was like living in New York City.

She was only too happy to oblige. If there was one thing Amber loved, it was an audience. Especially an audience who happened to be very cute, though he didn't seem to know it.

Her hand clasped firmly in Jeremy's, Amber began talking. She was still weak from the attack and, in truth, didn't feel well at all. But Bess had already told her she might be transferred to another hospital. If this young doctor was going to be her safety net, she couldn't think about how sick she was feeling. She had to latch on to him while she had the chance. So she talked.

Soap operas weren't Jeremy's thing, and he'd never seen the show. But he'd watch now. This gorgeous girl would be leaving the hospital soon enough when they found out what was wrong with her. It was comforting to know that after she left, he could still catch her on television five days a week. And maybe he'd even go to New York to see her. It wasn't that far. The way she was acting toward him, she might be glad to have him come visit her.

She's treating you this way, a nasty little inner voice told him, because she thinks you're a *doctor*. Or about to be, anyway. Wait till she finds out you're still a high school student and have no plans whatsoever to go into medicine. Tell her the truth *now*, while she's in a good mood. Tell her now, while she still thinks you saved her life. Tell her now, before someone else tells her.

"Amber . . ." Jeremy began.

But she interrupted. She squeezed his hand and, smiling brilliantly, said, "Oh, what's the matter with me? Here I am, rambling on and on about being a famous actress, and I haven't asked you a thing about what it's like being a doctor. An almost-doctor, anyway." She sat up and leaned closer to him. "Tell me again about the mansion you're going to build up on a hill."

Heady from the attentions of this beautiful girl, Jeremy forgot the voice in his head and carefully, enthusiastically, described in great detail Linden Hall, where Susannah Grant, not Jeremy, lived with her family.

"He's going to be okay, Mom, I know he is!" Abby assured her mother as they moved to the waiting room at Miller. "You heard the doctors. His burns aren't that bad."

"I also heard," Charlie O'Connor replied, "that he's in danger of developing pulmonary edema, pneumonia, or bronchitis from all that smoke in his lungs."

"Well, he won't! He just won't, that's all."

Abby glanced around the waiting room, frowning. "I wonder where Sid went?"

"More incoming!" Astrid called out to Susannah when she emerged from the examination room she'd been straightening. "People are getting too close to the fire, trying to save things from their homes. I just talked to Will on the radio. They're bringing in a woman who ran back inside her burning house to get a photo album, and had the stairs collapse under her. And we've got a teenager who tried to carry out his computer. He tripped over a cord and hit his head on a metal stair railing. Probable concussion. We've got trauma rooms C and F empty, right?"

Susannah nodded, but went to double-check. She was glad Will was coming in on this run. He needed a break. He'd been out there all day. On that last run, when he brought in two firemen who'd been overcome with smoke, he'd looked really gray. Maybe someone should check him out to see how much smoke *he* was inhaling. Besides, if he rested for a little bit, he'd be away from the fire, and she could quit worrying about something horrible happening to him, at least for a little while.

When Amber's agent and manager returned to the suite and suggested that Amber really should rest, Jeremy had no choice. Sliding his hand free of Amber's, he stood up reluctantly.

"You'll come back tonight, right?" she asked eagerly, reaching up to fluff the thick cloud of dark hair. "Unless . . . unless of course you have a date. It *is* Saturday night."

"No," he said quickly, "no date." Then he didn't like the way that sounded, and added, "I wasn't sure I'd be off tonight, so I didn't make any plans. Sure, I'll come back. If you don't think you'll be too tired to talk."

"Amber . . ." the agent said warningly.

"I absolutely won't be too tired," the actress said defiantly. "I'll nap now, and then I'll be wide awake when you come back."

And Jeremy left the suite feeling ten feet tall.

To find Callie Matthews lying in wait for him in the hallway.

He had barely closed the door when she sprang up from her chair and said nastily, *"Doctor* Noone? *Doctor?"*

chapter
14

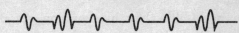

The first time Jeremy ever saw Callie, at a football game between their private day school and Grant High, he'd been impressed. With all that long, wavy hair, he'd thought she was awfully pretty. Now he just thought she was pretty awful. He had watched her snub people, gossip about them, and use them. One Friday night last spring, at a dance the hospital auxiliary had given, he had overheard her telling a nice, quiet girl named Sandy that she had seen Sandy's steady boyfriend with another girl the night before. When Sandy's boyfriend denied it, Sandy called him a liar and went home in tears. The next thing Jeremy knew, Callie was dancing in the boyfriend's arms, a satisfied smile on her face. Jeremy decided then and there that he would trust a cobra before he'd ever trust Callie Matthews.

Now, here she was, standing in front of him, hands on her hips, eyes narrowed, the only person who knew he'd lied to Amber Taylor about being an intern. If the person in front of him was

Susannah Grant or Kate Thompson or Abby O'Connor, he'd explain and they'd understand why he'd done it. They might even agree to keep his secret if he promised to tell Amber the truth himself.

But not Callie. Not in a million years. He could tell by the hungry look in her eyes that this was going to cost him. One nasty way or another, Jeremy Barlow was going to pay.

He wasn't giving up without a fight. "Is it my fault she thought I was a doctor?" he asked with fake innocence, at the same time trying to ease his way around Callie.

She sidestepped swiftly, barring his path again. "Oh, right. So how come you didn't set her straight?"

"I was going to, but then she had that attack, and everything was so crazy, I just forgot about it."

Callie laughed with scorn. "She wasn't having an allergic reaction just now, *was* she, Jeremy? And I distinctly heard her call you 'doctor.' You never intended to set her straight." Her blue eyes were very cold. "You get me in to see her, or I'm blowing the whistle. I mean it, Jeremy. I'm going to be her new best friend while she's here. You *see* to it, or *I'll* see to it that the whole hospital knows what a liar you are."

The whole hospital . . . she was including, of course, his father, Chief of Cardiology. Great.

Just super. Jeremy had no trouble imagining the conversation: "I *work* at that hospital," his father would say in his best look-at-all-I-have-to-put-up-with voice. "I have to face those people every day. How do you think I feel, knowing they're all talking about my son the liar behind my back?"

Callie's father might be in charge of the hospital, but at this particular moment, *she* was in charge of Jeremy Barlow, and they both knew it. "That's all I have to do, get you in to see her, and you won't tell? How do I know *you* won't tell *her*?"

Callie laughed lightly. "Oh, Jeremy, you can tell her you're the man in the moon for all I care. Play your little games. Just get me in there. And don't be hanging around all the time. I need time alone with her so I can get to know her. Find out how she became a success and all that." Her eyes narrowed again. "If you hang around too much, I might slip up and call you plain old 'Jeremy.' She'd think it was weird that I wasn't calling you Dr. Noone, right?"

Right. He was already gambling that none of the staff would see him in there and say, "Oh, hi, Jeremy, how's your dad?" like they always did. As if *he* would know. They saw a lot more of his father than he did. Amber would wonder why they kept asking him about his father. If he had to, he supposed he could just tell her the truth, that his father worked here, too, but she'd think it was weird that he hadn't told her that in the beginning.

"Okay," he agreed, knowing he had no other choice, "but not now. She's tired. It'll have to wait until tomorrow."

Callie grimaced unpleasantly. "Tomorrow? Oh, no. Tonight! It's still early. She can nap now and then we'll come back and talk to her later. You can introduce us, then you can *leave*." She tossed her long, blonde hair and threw him a smile that left him cold. "There's not that much time, Jeremy. The minute they diagnose her, she'll be shipped off to one of the other hospitals. I want to see her *today*!"

She was holding all the cards, and the look on her face said she knew it.

"Okay," Jeremy said with a sigh. "Visiting hours. Seven-thirty." He glanced out the window as they began walking down the hall. Outside, smoke had darkened the late afternoon as if it were already winter. "If this hospital is still standing by then. I heard the fire's completely out of control. Maybe they'll have to evacuate all the patients."

"Oh, don't be silly, Jeremy!" Callie pushed the elevator button. "That fire is all the way over in Eastridge. It won't come here. It never does."

Jeremy didn't believe in "never." He had thought, once upon a time, that his mother would never leave, but she had. There wasn't any such thing as "never." But he didn't have the energy to argue with Callie. "Abby's father was hurt in that fire," he said as they stepped into the elevator.

Callie's eyebrows went up. "O'Connor's father? That family sure doesn't take very good care of itself, does it?" She was thinking about the recent flood that had nearly taken the lives of Abby's younger sisters. *Would* have taken their lives, if she herself hadn't rescued them from floodwaters. Abby had helped some, but she didn't swim half as well as Caleb Matthews's only child, who was the proud possessor of an entire shelf unit filled with trophies and ribbons from swim meets. Her picture was in the newspaper after that incident. "Heroine," the paper had called her. Well, it was true, wasn't it? Too bad fame was so fleeting. Hardly anyone, including Jeremy, apparently, remembered how brave she'd been, risking her own life to save Abby's silly younger sisters.

"I don't think Mr. O'Connor got caught in the fire deliberately, Callie," Jeremy said matter-of-factly.

"Is he okay?" Abby, out of gratitude for the flood rescue, had arranged several dates for Callie with some hunky football players from Grant. None of the dates had panned out — boys were such jerks — but Callie had no desire to see her source dried up because Abby O'Connor was grieving the loss of a parent.

"Don't know yet. I just heard one of the nurses talking when I passed the station earlier. We can stop in at ER on our way down and see how he is. Susannah wanted me to let her know how Amber was, anyway."

But when they got downstairs, the ER was chaotic. Nurses and volunteers were running from one room to another carrying oxygen canisters and gauze and medical charts, orderlies were pushing crash carts and EKG machines along the hallways, and paramedics in navy blue jackets were helping gray-faced, coughing, firemen into treatment cubicles.

"It's still spreading," Susannah called breathlessly when she ran from one of the rooms and saw Jeremy. "The fire — it's out of control! How's that actress?"

"Fine . . ."

But Susannah had already rounded a corner into another room.

While Jeremy and Callie were still standing just outside the elevator, Will and another paramedic, named Tom, came running in pushing a gurney.

"Fell off the roof at his house," Jeremy heard Will tell the head nurse as she ran to help. "He was hosing it down. I guess he forgot how slippery tiles can get when they're wet. As far as we can tell, there's no head injury. He said he landed on his stomach on a pile of wood. Simple fractures of both arms. Abdomen is tender in the upper-right quadrant, vitals pulse one-forty, respiration thirty and labored, BP one-oh-eight over eighty-nine."

The man's neck had been immobilized with a collar. Because of the injuries to both arms, an IV had been inserted into his lower left leg. He was conscious and complaining of chest pain. "Give me something for the pain," he groaned.

"You didn't give him any morphine, did you?" Astrid Thompson asked Will sharply as they hurried along the corridor toward a treatment room.

"I know better than that," Will answered almost as sharply. "He's too shocky. Anyway, we're not sure how serious his injuries are. We don't want to mask any symptoms."

"Pulse one-forty, respiration thirty-six and shallow, BP seventy over fifty," Will's partner said urgently.

Nurse Thompson bent over the patient. "Sir? Sir, could you have hit that pile of logs with your chest instead of your stomach?"

But the man could only repeat, "Please, something for the pain. My arms . . ."

Watching as the gurney disappeared around a

corner, Callie said, without emotion, "Well, at least he didn't get burned. Wouldn't that be horrible?" She shuddered.

"I guess breaking both arms and smashing your chest on a pile of logs wouldn't be any picnic, either," Jeremy said flatly. Callie was hopeless. And now she was going to ruin everything for him with Amber. He had actually had a chance to get to know a gorgeous, talented, famous girl until Callie showed up with her blackmailing scheme. She'd probably never let him have five minutes alone with Amber.

Why couldn't Callie be on that gurney instead of some poor guy who'd probably never even thought about blackmailing anyone?

Not at all ashamed of the thought, Jeremy said, "Maybe you should go home and hose down your roof, Callie. Just in case." He was only half-kidding.

"Very funny. I'm going home to change into something really sophisticated. I don't want Amber thinking I'm some stupid hick who's never opened a fashion magazine." Callie fixed cold blue eyes on Jeremy. "But I *will* be back here at seven-thirty, Jeremy, fire or no fire, and you'd better be here, too."

"Some of the roads might be closed," he said, hope in his voice. "You heard Susannah. The fire's out of control. There are probably cops everywhere, telling people to stay home."

"*Be* here," she ordered. Tossing her head the way only Callie could do, she turned on her heel and hurried to the door.

Both of Damon's hands were thickly bandaged, and a swath of white gauze covered his left cheek as well. His lower left leg was covered with another thick layer of white. When it had been decided that he had no serious lung damage, he had been given a mild sedative and admitted to the fourth floor. Although he was sitting up in bed in his hospital room, he wasn't sitting up very straight, and his eyes were beginning to cloud.

"You should lie down," Kate told him. The nurse, trying to keep abreast of the constant flow of patients, had moved on to another room, leaving Kate to see that Damon was comfortable. "You're going to be really sleepy in a few minutes. You don't want to sleep sitting up, do you?"

"I don't want to sleep at all." His voice, coming from a throat rubbed raw by smoke, was barely audible, but he sounded angry. "I want to get back to work."

"You've done your bit already." Kate pulled the white bedspread up to his waist, careful not to let it rub against any burned areas. "You're a hero, Lawrence. Relax and enjoy it." She checked his water pitcher. It was full. "Anyway, how much help would you be at the fire with both hands bandaged?"

He slid down in the bed. "C'mon over here," he croaked sleepily, trying and failing to focus his eyes well enough to leer at her, "and I'll *show* you what I can do with both hands bandaged."

Kate couldn't help laughing. He didn't look the least bit threatening. With his eyes clouded and his features relaxed, he reminded her of their dog, Lancelot, after he had been tranquilized at the vet's. If Damon should try to stand up now, his legs would fold beneath him just like Lancelot's, and he'd fall to the floor in a heap. "Get some rest," she ordered, walking over to stand beside his bed, adjusting his bedding for the third time and wishing she could think of something else she could do to make him more comfortable.

Damon crooked a finger at Kate. "C'mere," he whispered. "Need to tell you something. It's important."

Kate looked down at him with suspicion. "I don't trust you. Just say whatever it is. I can hear you."

He shook his head. "Gotta bend down. Don't want anybody else to hear."

"There's no one else in here," Kate said stubbornly. But she bent down, deciding that the sooner she let him say whatever it was, the sooner he'd relax and go to sleep. Sleep was what he needed.

She wasn't at all prepared for what happened next. Instead of whispering in her ear, Damon lifted one bandaged hand and placed it on the back of her head, gently pulling her face closer to his, and kissed her. Not a light, casual peck, or a friendly well-hey-how-are-you kiss, or a thanks-for-taking-care-of-me kiss. In spite of Damon's obvious drowsiness, the kiss he gave her was definitely one of those if-I-don't-kiss-you-right-now-I'm-going-to-go-nuts kisses.

The tingle that Kate had told herself she imagined earlier increased in voltage. When she finally pulled away and stood upright, all she could say was, "What was *that* for?"

"That was just for starters," he said groggily, and reached out for her hand. His felt warm and amazingly strong in view of how drugged he was. "More later. Don' go 'way. . . ."

His eyes closed.

Oh boy, Kate thought, as, still holding his hand, she sank into the chair beside his bed. I think I'm in trouble here. This is *not* good.

So why was it, then, that it *felt* so good?

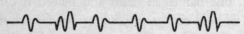

Jeremy left the hospital only once that day, briefly, to buy a balloon bouquet for Amber. He would take it to her during evening visiting hours. Maybe she'd be so pleased, she would ignore Callie and talk only to him. Then Callie wouldn't dare kick him out of the suite.

He was astonished by how dark it was outside. Though the fire was still on the other side of the river, the thick, gray smoke and the pungent smell accompanying it lay across the city like a dirty blanket. Traffic was so snarled, he couldn't get across the main highway. Impossible. He finally parked his car and walked to the mall a few blocks away, only to find it closed. A large metal sign on the door had been hand-printed with the words, CLOSED DUE TO THREAT OF FIRE. He read it three times, with eyes burning from the foul air.

"*What* threat of fire?" he muttered, annoyed, but also uneasy. Did the people who managed the mall really think the fire would jump the river? The refinery was located on the edge of

Eastridge for a reason. Putting it clear over there kept any fires away from the heart of town, away from Med Center and the libraries and the office buildings and the shops. And away from the west side of town, where the nicer homes were. Like *his*.

The unfairness of that didn't escape Jeremy — after all, why should Eastridge be in harm's way instead of some other neighborhood? But the truth was, he had always felt a certain sense of safety because the refinery *was* so far away. Every summer, when the fires hit, he could, if he chose, climb to the top of the hill behind his house and gaze out across the city to watch the smoke and flames, secure in the knowledge that nothing of his was in danger. It was a little like watching a movie. Except that the fire was real.

The traffic was even worse when Jeremy made his way back to Emsee. When he crossed the highway on foot, dodging between cars that weren't moving, he could see off to his right the faint blue of a police car's rooftop siren. An accident. Probably more than one, if you asked him, because how could any driver *see* in all this thick, black smoke? It was worse than fog.

He was careful to avoid ER upon his return to the hospital. If the traffic problems he'd seen were any indication, the place would be a zoo, what with fire victims and traffic accident victims at the same time. He went in through the lobby instead, straight to the elevators. On a night like this, he couldn't help being glad that he had never let Susannah or Abby talk him into volunteering at the hospital. The excuse he'd given them was that he didn't have time. The real truth was, he knew everyone he met there would compare him to his handsome, dynamic father, and Jeremy would come up short. Who needed that?

The elevator doors slid open and Jeremy stepped inside, on his way to see Amber. He was hoping like mad that Callie wouldn't show up. If she'd left the hospital to change her clothes, like she'd planned, maybe she wouldn't be able to get back, because of the smoke and the traffic. Then he could have Amber all to himself, which was exactly what he wanted.

Downstairs, in ER, the encroaching smoke had sent one traffic victim after another in for treatment. Sometimes the victims arrived in twos and threes. It would have to have been insane to speed when visibility was almost nil, so most of the injuries were relatively minor. But they still had to be tended to.

And then there were those people who had insisted on trying to save their homes. Some had fallen from ladders, some had been cut by glass when windows exploded from the intense heat, others were suffering from minor smoke inhalation damage. A teenager had inadvertently got in the way of a fire hose and been slammed up against the brick wall of his house by the tremendous force of the water. The collision had shattered an elbow and broken his right leg.

"The waiting room is full," Astrid informed Susannah and Kate when they returned from grabbing a quick cup of coffee and a bagel in the cafeteria. She handed Kate a hefty collection of medical charts. "Most of these new charts haven't been touched yet, and we've got several people who should be seen right away. None of the staff has had dinner yet, and no one's had time to check the crash carts or restock any of the cabinets. We're low on linens, gauze, saline, and suture supplies. I haven't had any luck getting housekeeping or supply up here to restock, so you'll have to do it. Kate, you handle that. Get an orderly to help you. Susannah, take these charts into the waiting room and get as much information as you can. Nurse Connie Brewer's already in there. She can decide who needs to be treated first. When you've finished with the charts, come see me."

While she was speaking, paramedics arrived with three traffic accident victims. The first clearly had a serious chest injury. He was dispatched immediately to X Ray. The second had a broken nose and two serious facial lacerations, requiring the services of a plastic surgeon, summoned by telephone. The third, a teenager, had no visible injuries beyond a rapidly blackening eye, but was unconscious. He was steered rapidly to an examination room.

"It's nasty out there," Will said hurriedly to Susannah as he passed with the third gurney. "Can't see two feet in front of you because of the smoke. All of our runs are taking way too long, but it wouldn't do anyone any good if we crashed into a tree, would it?"

Oh, great, Susannah thought, making her way to the waiting room. As if the fire wasn't enough to worry about. Now they had a serious traffic hazard on their hands, too.

She was *not* going to obsess about Will being out in horrendous traffic conditions. No way. She had work to do. She couldn't be distracted with worry over him. Put him out of her mind, that's what she had to do.

Sure.

Susannah hesitated in the doorway of the waiting room. When she and Kate left to go downstairs for coffee, there had only been four people waiting for treatment. Now there wasn't an empty seat.

Nurse Brewer was already inside, moving quickly from one patient to another, assessing their injuries and taking notes on a small notepad. She summoned Susannah to her side and began speaking rapidly. "The lacerations over there," she said, pointing to a young girl with her hands to her face, bright red showing through her splayed fingers, "goes to a suture room right *now*. The cuts aren't deep and she's not in shock, but she's been waiting far too long. Over there, against the wall, get information from that elderly gentleman about how far he fell from the ladder he was on. He seems a little disoriented and may have a concussion, although he insists he's fine. I'm not sure about him. If he can't tell you how far he fell, get an orderly to put him on a gurney and take him upstairs for a CAT scan."

Susannah was writing on her own notepad as fast as she could, trying at the same time to keep the cluster of medical charts from slipping out from under her arm.

"I think the lady in the pink dress sitting in the corner over there might have smoke damage," Nurse Brewer continued. "She's coughing up a storm, and she said she stayed in her house because she thought it wouldn't burn if she was in it. Something about her being a really lucky person, someone bad things never happen to. Doesn't make any sense, so she might have a touch of carbon monoxide. It'll do that, make you think things that make no sense. She's probably going to need an EKG and a chest X ray. Take her as soon as there's a room free, okay?"

Susannah felt completely overwhelmed. That

feeling worsened when Nurse Brewer said, "Okay, I'm outa here. Dr. Izbecki needs me to help with that kid who got in the way of the hose. It sounds like he broke practically every bone in his body. Do what you can here. If I find anyone wandering around with nothing to do, I'll send them in."

They both knew she wasn't going to find anyone like that.

Susannah, using the notes she had hastily taken, did the best she could. Joey Rudd, the only orderly who wasn't otherwise occupied, brought wheelchairs for those who needed them, and helped Susannah assist the elderly gentleman onto a gurney. Joey volunteered to wheel it upstairs for the CAT scan of his brain. One woman, with a laceration on her forehead, spoke no English. Susannah was forced to resort to her high school Spanish, which wasn't very good, to start the woman's medical chart. A lot of spaces were left empty. She had no idea what the Spanish word for *insurance* might be.

When Kate had finished the restocking, she came to help.

"How's that fireman?" Susannah asked, handing Kate a batch of charts. "The one who rescued Abby's father?" She hadn't talked to Abby since the family had left for the burn unit, and had no idea how Mr. O'Connor was doing. She would have to call Miller the very first chance she got. If she ever got one.

"Damon?" Kate shrugged. "Sleeping." Remembering the kiss, she felt heat rising in her face.

Susannah glanced at her sharply. "That's not much of an answer. How *is* he? How bad were his burns?"

"He'll be okay." Kate surveyed the waiting room. There were a few empty seats now, but plenty of people remained in various degrees of discomfort waiting for treatment. "Who's next?"

"You must like that fireman a lot," Susannah said knowingly, "or you wouldn't be avoiding talking about him." She pointed discreetly toward the elderly Spanish woman. "Nurse Barrow put her next on the list, if there's a suture room open. How's your Spanish?"

"My Spanish is pretty good." Kate fixed a level gaze on her friend. "As for the fireman you're so worried about, I have better things to do right now than discuss Damon Lawrence with you."

Susannah laughed. "Yes, *ma'am*! Class will now come to order."

Kate laughed then, too. "Okay, okay, so I sounded like a teacher. Sorry. But, come on, you have to admit we've got our hands full here. No time for conversation, right?"

"That means there *is* something to talk about. I *knew* it! Later, okay?"

But as Kate strode away and began speaking in rapid Spanish to the elderly woman, Susannah wondered if she would ever hear about the fireman from Kate. If Kate was going to confide in anyone, it probably wouldn't be her. They were friends, but no one could call them close. She had tried, because she liked and admired Kate Thompson. It was funny how Kate made fun of Will's pride, but didn't even seem to realize that her own kept people at a safe distance, too.

Look who's talking, Susannah scolded herself silently. When was the last time *you* confided in someone? Have you ever told Kate how scared you are that you're not going to be able to hack it here in Emergency? Have you ever told Will you wish he'd call you some evening so the two of you could talk for longer than a minute or two?

That's true, Susannah thought. Even Abby doesn't know how I feel about Will, how I *really* feel about him, because I've never admitted it. That's too scary. Just like Kate won't say how attracted she is to that fireman. Because it's scaring *her*.

At the fire site firemen, alarmed by the accidental pummeling of the young man by a fire hose, ordered all of the volunteers away.

Sam protested vehemently, but Sid wheeled

his chair backward without an argument. "I've got to get back to Abby," he told Sam emphatically. "I'm not doing that much good here, and I have to know that she's okay. Take me to Emsee?"

"Okay," Sam agreed reluctantly, "but I'm coming right back here." His handsome face was smoke-grimed, the vicious wind had tangled his blonde hair, and the rims of his eyes were inflamed. "I can't just sit around and watch the city burn down."

As they moved away and he glanced over his shoulder at the fire scene, it seemed to him that Grant very well could burn to the ground in this, the worst refinery fire ever.

chapter
16

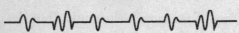

When Jeremy stepped out of the elevator on the fourth floor, his good mood vanished. Callie was already there, impatiently striding back and forth in the hallway. She was wearing a chic blue velvet pantsuit and heeled boots. Her blonde hair was pulled back in a sophisticated upsweep.

The only thing missing, Jeremy thought darkly, *is a tiara. Queen Callie, here to take away my chance to be alone with a gorgeous girl who likes me.*

"Well, it's about time! Where have you been? They wouldn't let me inside." She sent him a baleful stare. "*You're* the only one with pull around here. *Dr.* Noone."

Jeremy flushed, but answered coolly, "Yeah, well, just remember that you need me, Callie. And don't go saying anything stupid in front of Amber. If I get tossed out, so do you."

Callie Matthews was not above using people. She had, in fact, made it common practice. But using them when she *chose*, and *needing* them to help her out were two very different things. She hated the latter. Being at Jeremy's mercy left a bitter, coppery taste in her mouth. Well, it wouldn't last. She'd make friends with Amber quickly, then she wouldn't need Jeremy anymore. "Just get me inside," she snapped. "I'll take care of the rest."

Amber did *not* seem happy to see Jeremy in the company of another pretty girl. But within seconds, Callie was gushing over her like a waterfall, and if there was anything Amber succumbed to faster than applause, it was an ardent fan.

"I haven't missed a single show since you came on," Callie oozed, "and my friends and I all agree that Lynette is the best character *A New Day* has ever had!"

Amber's meticulously plucked eyebrows raised. Patting the chair beside her bed, she said, "You haven't missed a single show? Really? Come and sit down and tell me what you like best about Lynette."

Jeremy glowered in the background as Callie hurried to the chair and slid into place. The two girls immediately launched into a discussion of recent plotlines on the soap opera. I should have known, he told himself bitterly. Me, alone with a beautiful, famous actress, was too good to be true. If I were so great that someone like Amber Taylor would be interested in me, I'd be as popular as Sam Grant, wouldn't I? I'd be constantly dating the most gorgeous, popular girls in town. I'd be at a different party every night. And if I were that interesting, my mother probably wouldn't have left.

But just as Jeremy was beginning to sink into a pit of despair, Amber suddenly remembered exactly where her interests might lie if she lost her job. This Callie-person, though she was a great fan, couldn't do a thing for her. But Dr. Noone could. She interrupted Callie right in the middle of a sentence to lift her head and say, "Oh, Jeremy, tell me, how's that awful fire? Did they put it out?"

Insulted by her rudeness, Callie jerked upright, her eyes narrowing.

Jeremy, his face brightening, moved quickly to stand beside the bed. "No, it's not out, but you don't have to worry. You're safe here. I won't let anything happen to you."

"Oh, gag," Callie murmured, her mouth twisting nastily.

Startled, Amber looked at her. "What?"

Callie smiled brightly. "Nothing. We were talking about that scene a couple of weeks ago when you found out that Tony was seeing someone behind your back, remember?"

But it was too late. Amber had remembered what her future might hold in store for her and she wasn't going to forget it again. Ignoring Callie, she focused all of her attention on "Dr. Noone."

Jeremy beamed, while Callie fumed.

When Sam had dropped Sid off at Rehab and returned to the fire, Sid sat in his wheelchair at the entrance, studying the woods behind the big brick building. The trees along the riverbank were old and huge, their branches, still fully-leafed out, bending toward the water.

The danger was, he noticed as the warm but wild wind battered him, the trees on *both* sides of the river were bending toward each *other*. Some of the branches were touching branches on the opposite side. If the fire came close enough, it could jump the river with no problem at all.

As far as he knew, that had never happened before. But then, the last serious fire had been over ten years ago, and the trees would have been smaller. Maybe their branches hadn't met in the middle of the river that long ago.

Turning his wheelchair to move it up the ramp into Rehab, Sid wondered what hospital personnel would say if he suggested they send a crew out to cut down some of those trees. They'd probably think he was nuts.

But that pink-orange glow, seen dimly to the east through the thick haze of smoke that hung in the air, seemed to Sid to be much closer now than it had been when Sam first lifted him out of the van.

The first thing he intended to do when he got inside was call the burn unit and see how Abby's father was. Maybe one of the nurses would let him talk to her, see if she wanted him to come on over. He didn't want to get in the way, but he hated the idea of not being there when she was feeling down.

But he hadn't been inside Rehab more than a second or two when a nurse named Kathy called to him, "Have you seen Billy Griffin? I can't find him anywhere."

Billy Griffin was only eight and a half, a rambunctious little kid with red hair and freckles who'd slammed his new bicycle into the back of a bakery truck one day last summer. He hadn't been wearing a helmet, although, his mother told the doctors, she had insisted that he do so. It was a severe head injury, but he had survived. Now he had to learn everything all over again, just like a newborn. He had to be taught how to walk, talk, tie his shoes, brush his teeth, feed himself, even had to relearn the alphabet and how to count. And from what Sid had seen and heard, little Billy was a difficult student. Impatient and restless, and angry most of the time. He had run away from Rehab three times, but his parents always brought him back. Now, he usually just hid somewhere on the premises.

"Haven't seen him," Sid answered. "But I haven't been here. I was over at the fire."

"Oh, that's finally out. We just got word."

Sid was more surprised than relieved. The fire was out? Then what was that glow he'd seen across the river? Must have been his imagination.

"I can't find him anywhere," the nurse continued. "He was scheduled for physical therapy at six this evening, but said he had a bad headache. I let him take a nap." Guilt flashed across her pale, narrow face. "I know I'm not supposed to let him off the hook like that, but he really didn't look well. He said he'd had his window open and he thought he'd inhaled some of the smoke. I told him to sleep while I went to dinner, but when I went back up half an hour ago, he wasn't in his room. I've been looking all over for him, and I can't find him anywhere."

"I'll help you look," Sid offered. "Soon as I make a quick phone call, okay?"

The nurse had already gone back down the hall, a worried frown on her face.

"Yes," Abby said when Sid finally got her on the phone, "I'd love it if you'd come over here. Everyone's so nervous about the fire, and they've got new patients coming in all the time. It's a madhouse. Almost as bad as ER." She lowered her voice. "I miss you. Where have you been?"

"At the fire. I just heard it's out, though. How's your dad?"

"They say he's doing okay. He looks awful. A lot of his hair was burned off, and his face has red patches all over it. The worst of it is on his back, though, so he has to lie on his stomach and we have to crouch down to talk to him. He's sleeping right now. Are you coming over?"

"In a sec. Billy Griffin's missing again. I said I'd help look for him. Shouldn't take long. I know most of his favorite hiding places. He was in the third-floor linen closet last time, so he won't be there this time. Maybe the library. Don't go away, okay?"

"I won't. Hurry, though, okay? I really need to see you."

As he always did when he talked to Abby, Sid hung up with a feeling of contentment. She hadn't said she loved him, but more and more lately he was allowing himself to believe that could be true. There was something about the way she looked at him, the way she seemed so happy when he was with her . . . maybe she did love him.

Wouldn't that be something?

He was replacing the receiver, smiling to himself, when Kathy appeared at his side again. "Billy's not here anywhere," she said. "He's gone!"

"Are you sure? Did you check the laundry rooms and the library? What about the kitchen? He likes that walk-in pantry."

"I checked them all. So did security." She waved a hand toward the door. "I can't believe he's out there, in *that*. All that smoke, and that wind is awful. He shouldn't be out in that, Sid."

"Did you send security after him?"

Kathy nodded. "They went to his house to check. But I don't see how anyone can find him in *this*. People can't even see to drive. What if he went into the woods?"

Sid remembered then: Billy telling him in his oddly disjointed sentences that whenever the weather was nice, he sneaked out into the woods where he was building a tree house, "up tall." He had said angrily, several weeks ago, "I stay here. I make fun place me." Sid interpreted that to mean that if Billy had to stay in this place he hated, he was at least going to build a little hideaway for himself. A fun place to be. A tree house in the woods. "Up tall" probably meant in one of the taller trees.

Sid hadn't thought about it much at the time. He wasn't sure Billy was physically capable of climbing even a small tree, never mind one "up tall." Besides, he didn't think Billy could get his hands on any tools, and he was equally certain that the little boy wouldn't find it so easy to leave the building. The staff tended to keep a closer watch on chronic runaways.

But now . . .

"I'll go take a look around outside," he told

the frantic nurse. "Maybe he changed his mind about leaving and came back. Could be hanging around out there, afraid to come back in because he knows he screwed up again."

Kathy looked relieved. She reached out to ruffle Sid's dark, wavy hair. "You're adorable," she said, "you know that? That Abby is *such* a lucky girl." She sighed heavily. "I guess I'd better go call Billy's parents. That's a conversation I dread. His father will say, 'Can't you people keep an eye on one small boy?' But I can't put it off forever. Just let me know right away if he's out there, okay? Maybe their line will be busy and by the time I get through, you'll be dragging Billy back inside. Thanks, Sid."

Sid felt a stab of trepidation. She was counting on him, expecting him to deliver so that she wouldn't have to face Billy's parents. But he had no idea where Billy's "tree house" might be out there in those woods. "Up tall" . . . what did that mean? Tall, sure, but *where*?

Abby was waiting for him at the burn unit. He'd promised her he'd be right there, but there was an eight-year-old out there somewhere, a kid who wouldn't realize how disorienting thick smoke could be. If he really did have a tree house — probably no more than a bunch of logs piled together — maybe he had run out to check on it, make sure there were no flames around it anywhere. Unless the smoke had thinned since Sid came into the building, Billy could easily have become lost out there, unable to see his way back to Rehab. He could be wandering around, scared half to death.

Instead of heading for one of the enclosed passageways that would take Sid directly to the burn unit to meet Abby, he turned his wheelchair in the direction of the door.

Abby would understand. That could be her little brother Mattie out there, right? And Sid would certainly go hunting for *him.*

As soon as the doors swung open, he realized that the smoke *hadn't* thinned. On the contrary, it was so thick now that he could barely make out the outlines of the other hospitals in the complex.

"Billy?" he called as he eased his chair down the ramp. "Billy Griffin? You out here?" Swallowing a cough, Sid hoped the theory he'd expressed to Kathy was correct. If Billy really was lurking out here near the entrance, Sid would assure him that he wasn't going to be punished, and they'd both go back inside, away from this putrid cloud of foul-smelling smoke. "Billy? Come on out now, kid, it's okay. No one's mad at you. Let's get back inside, okay? This air'll kill us. Billy?"

But the only sound Sid heard was a pair of sirens.

chapter
17

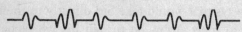

When Billy Griffin didn't answer, Sid sat in his wheelchair in front of the Rehab building, studying the woods lying directly ahead of him. In the middle of a warm day, with the sun shining on his back and shoulders, he might have enjoyed a brief trip through the thick forest. But at night, with the late-evening darkness intensified by the smoke hanging in the air, taking a wheelchair along those pine-needled paths would be no easy task.

"Billy! Where *are* you?"

No answer.

Sid lectured himself: Let security look for the kid. That's their job. Not yours.

But security didn't know about the tree house, did they? If there *was* one. "Up tall," Billy had said. The tallest trees were along the riverbank behind Rehab. Their branches leaned precariously out across the Revere River. The darkness and the thick smoke would make it impossible for Billy to see where a branch ended. That, combined with his lack of motor coordination, could cause him to fall into the cold, rushing water.

Sid made up his mind. Taking a deep breath, he rolled the wheelchair forward, into the woods.

"It's out." One of the firemen on East Sixtieth Street yanked his helmet off and wiped his grimy face with a handkerchief. "It's finally out. We just got a call from the guys in the woods. They're keeping an eye on a few hot spots, making sure they don't flare up again, but the fire itself is out. We got the news out already. People were waiting. I called Med Center myself." He sagged gratefully against the fire truck parked in front of a row of houses. None of them had burned, but all were gray with smoke.

Sam glanced around him. "It's out? But the smoke . . ."

"That's just residue. It'll take awhile for it to clear out. Coupla days, maybe." The fireman turned toward Sam and his friends. They were all filthy. Their eyes were so red, they seemed to glow in the dark. "Gotta thank you guys for your help. You saved this block, anyway." He peered more closely at Sam. "Aren't you Sam Grant? You don't even live in this neighborhood. Mighty big of you to risk your neck for people you don't know."

Sam thought of Will and Kate. He wasn't as close to them as Susannah was, but he liked both of them. "I know a few. You sure it's out?"

"Positive. We'll be keeping an eye on those hot spots. And people won't be able to come back into the area until the smoke clears. But it's out, all right." The fireman shook his head. His eyes, too, were red-rimmed. "Wasn't sure we were going to get this one under contol. What saved us was, the oil tanks didn't blow, so the fire was confined to the office buildings on the site, and then the neighborhood. The wind actually did us a favor, blowing the flames away from the tanks and into Eastridge instead. Too bad about the houses. But if the tanks had gone up in flames, too, we wouldn't be standing here talking right now."

Sam would have looked then to see if Will's and Kate's houses were still standing, but he had no idea where either of them lived. He wondered if Susannah did.

He should call her, maybe tell her he'd helped out a little. Let her know that she wasn't the only person in the family who cared about people. Sure, he liked to have a good time. Why not? But that didn't mean he didn't care about people.

A party . . . Sam laughed softly to himself. They should have a party tonight to celebrate conquering the fire. A Saving-of-the-City celebration. They could have it at the hospital, maybe. They'd had parties there before, usually in the ballroom at Rehab. He'd mention it to Susannah, see what she thought.

But when Sam called Emsee on the cellular phone in his van, the nurse who answered said crisply, "I'm sorry, but Ms. Grant is much too busy to come to the telephone. We've got our hands full over here. Unless this is an emegency, you'll have to call back later."

Probably thinks I'm one of Susannah's boyfriends, Sam thought, amused, and hung up. He could have told the nurse he was Samuel Grant's only son. She'd have put him through to Susannah so fast, the phone lines would have sizzled. But he only used that tactic when he was desperate. He'd just go on over there, and suggest a party. Then he'd go home and take the longest, hottest shower in the history of the universe, and come back for the festivities when he looked human again.

Thinking "party," Sam was in high spirits as he drove himself and his pals to Med Center.

"Paramedic down," Astrid said crisply when Susannah, arms filled with clean linens, ran into the treatment room where the head nurse was preparing a fresh suture tray. "We just got word. They're on their way with him now."

Susannah stopped short, her face draining of color. "*Which* paramedic?"

"I don't know yet." Astrid looked up from the

tray. "The fire's out. But some guy over in East-ridge thought that meant he could go back inside his house, even though it was still smoldering. The firemen didn't see him sneak in, but one of the paramedics did, and ran after him. Forgot all about the rules at a fire, I guess. Anyway, the floor collapsed beneath both of them. They're bringing them in now. That's all I know."

Susannah's knees threatened to buckle. Will. Will was out there, Will was a paramedic, Will would have seen the danger when that man entered his house. Will might have, just for a second, forgotten or ignored the rule about no paramedics entering fire sites. They were supposed to leave that to the firemen. "You don't . . ." she began shakily, "you don't think it's Will, do you?"

Astrid's eyes were sympathetic. "I don't know, Susannah. They didn't say." She glanced around the room. "Let's get on out there and be ready for the ambulance. They said ETA was about four minutes."

Susannah moved stiffly, a windup doll with an expression of dread on her face. She winced when she stepped outside and the odor of smoke hit her, stinging her eyes. The fire was out . . . hadn't Astrid said that? Hadn't she said the fire was out? That was good news. News that should have sent relief washing over her like a tide of warm water.

But the words *paramedic down* were getting in the way.

She heard the siren, its eerie, haunting wail approaching from the east. And then another, right behind it. They'd brought them in two separate ambulances? Did that mean the injuries were so serious, one ambulance couldn't handle more than one patient at a time?

Oh, God, Susannah breathed silently, please don't let it be Will, please don't. I have to tell him how I feel, please. . . .

The first ambulance held the man who had entered his house after it had burned. He was unconscious and was being given CPR by one of the paramedics as he was lifted from the back of the ambulance.

None of the three paramedics was Will Jackson.

An understanding Astrid said, "You stay here and wait for the second victim. I'll go on inside with this one. He's critical."

Susannah, her knees shaking, held her breath as the rear doors to the second ambulance swung open. . . .

And Will jumped down. In one piece. Arms and legs intact, moving in his usual brisk, competent way. He was okay. He hadn't entered the house, hadn't fallen through the floor. . . .

Susannah exhaled. She felt tears of relief springing to her eyes and didn't care if anyone noticed. She wanted to rush to Will and throw her arms around his neck and shout, "You're okay, you're okay! You're not hurt!"

She knew she couldn't do that. This was not the time. She'd learned her lesson, though. Now that the fire was out, if she didn't do anything else before this day was over, she was going to tell Will, straight out, how frightened she'd been when she thought he'd been hurt . . . or worse. Even if he didn't want to know. Even if he didn't care. She was *going* to tell him.

Then they brought the stretcher out, and she saw that the paramedic was an older man named Donny. He had a huge gash at the temple, bleeding profusely into the gauze pad placed over it, and, Susannah realized as she saw the bone protruding from his left thigh, a bad fracture.

"Dumb move," he muttered as Will and Susannah and two other staff members whisked him inside and down the hall, "dumb move. I know better. Didn't think . . . should have my head examined."

Susannah, giddy with relief that Will was fine, laughed and said, "I think you're probably going to. I'll bet anything Dr. Izbecki orders a CAT scan. Maybe he'll let you look at the wiring up there, see what went wrong."

Will laughed. His eyes met hers, and she wondered if he was reading them correctly. Could he see how glad she was that he wasn't hurt? That he wasn't lying on the gurney instead of Donny? Abby had said, more than once, that Susannah was an expert at hiding her feelings. Well, this was one time Susannah hoped that wasn't true. She *wanted* Will to see. That would have to be enough until both new patients had been taken care of and she had a chance to talk to him.

When Donny had been taken upstairs for the necessary surgery on his thigh, Susannah and Will went to check on the man who had returned to his house. He had failed to respond to CPR, and the room was a frenzy of activity. The bright red crash cart sat beside the table and Susannah could see five figures in white working around the table. The air of tension in the room stretched all the way to the threshhold, where she and Will stood uncertainly.

She saw a white strip of EKG paper rolling steadily toward the floor. She didn't know how to read the strips, and couldn't see the lines from where she stood, anyway. But she guessed that there was little or no activity on it when she realized that Dr. Izbecki was vigorously massaging the man's heart in an effort to get it started.

Astrid Thompson stood beside the crash cart, selecting various medications as Dr. Izbecki snapped out a request for them. She lined them up in order of the request, making it easier for him to select the necessary syringe as needed. Another nurse stood back from the table with paper and pen, recording each medication used and the amount, while a third nurse concentrated on the heart monitor, reciting aloud the results in a flat, unemotional voice.

Susannah and Will watched in complete silence the intensive efforts to resuscitate the man. They seemed to go on forever.

"Breathe, man!" Dr. Izbecki shouted, "breathe! Fire or no fire, no one's dying on my shift tonight."

Susannah saw the intubation instruments lying on a small table to Dr. Izbecki's left. At one end was the long, straight steel blade that pushed the tongue aside before putting the tube in. Beside that lay a white endotracheal tube. If the doctor had to intubate to enable the man to breathe, he would have to push the tube far down inside the patient's throat, to the top of the lungs. Then the patient could be connected to the respirator through a crazy circuit of plastic blue and clear tubes.

But that was a desperate measure for desperate cases, and if it happened, if the man needed a respirator to do his breathing for him, his chances weren't good.

Suddenly Dr. Izbecki stopped, stood back.

Susannah could see the monitor. A normal heart pattern was sliding across the screen.

A sigh of relief whispered around the room.

Susannah reached out and took Will's hand.

She wasn't sure why, but she always felt like crying when someone was brought back like this. It was so . . . amazing.

When the patient had been stabilized, he was quickly moved upstairs to Intensive Care. He wasn't out of danger yet, Susannah knew that. But he was alive.

Lost in the drama, she had completely forgotten what it was she wanted to tell Will.

In the woods, Sid was having more trouble seeing than he'd anticipated. From his wheelchair on the path, he could barely make out the shadowy outlines of the trees flanking him on both sides. His eyes and throat burned fiercely. How long would it take for the smoke to clear? He couldn't stand much more of this. And if Billy really was out here, he'd been exposed longer. He'd have to be seen by a doctor when and if they found him. He could have lung damage.

Sid pulled the hem of his plaid shirt up over his nose and mouth, but the fabric was cotton, too thin to act as a barrier, and it already reeked of smoke because he'd been wearing it at the refinery site.

Through the thin material, he called hoarsely, "Billy? Billy Griffin?"

From high above came a voice — frightened, trembling, its usual bravado absent. "Sid? Sid, me up tall, you me down."

As relieved as he was to hear the voice, Sid sagged backward in his chair. Oh, great. Just great. He knew what that cryptic call meant: Sid, you get me down out of this tree.

And me in a wheelchair, Sid thought, shaking his head.

chapter
18

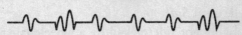

When her father had fallen asleep and her mother had gone home to check on the kids, Abby hiked through the enclosed passageways to Rehab. The heels of her black boots on the white tile stamped out her anger. You . . . said . . . you . . . would . . . be . . . right . . . there, the heels telegraphed. Aloud, she said, her words bouncing hollowly off the white, igloo-blocked walls, "*I* would have been there for *you*, Sid Costello!"

The reason Abby had commented on Susannah hiding her feelings was, Abby herself was just the opposite. Anyone passing her in the corridor could see her fury. Her dark curls bounced with every step she took, and her cheeks were the same red as her turtleneck sweater. Anyone passing her in the corridor would have been surprised, too. Abby O'Connor was known for her cheerful disposition. She kept insisting that she had a terrible temper, but no one at Rehab or Grant Memorial had yet seen it in action.

"That's because," she had told Kate and Susannah recently, "no one has ever let me down here at Emsee. That's what makes me maddest, when people say they'll do something, and then they don't do it. That sets me off like a rocket. And," she finished calmly, "people here don't do that."

Well, until *Sid*!

Probably got sidetracked by a wheelchair race, she thought angrily as she entered Rehab. Sid might not be on the football field these days, but he was one of the most competitive people she'd ever met. And he was forever attempting things no one at Rehab, including her, thought he was ready for. She understood his impatience, but she had been taught in her classes that getting better meant accepting your new limitations. Sid still wasn't willing to admit that he *had* any. Some of the doctors thought that was why he was making such speedy, impressive progress. Others stated aloud that he was just plain foolhardy. Abby agreed with both schools of thought.

It never occurred to her that Billy Griffin might still be missing.

"Where is Sid?" she demanded of one of the nurses. She did most of her volunteer work at Rehab, and knew everyone on the staff.

And they knew her *and* Sid, and had been following with affection and some amusement the romance between the two.

"I haven't seen him." The nurse came out

from behind the desk. "We've all been so busy hunting for Billy, I haven't kept track of where everyone else is."

A pang of guilt stabbed Abby. "They haven't found him yet? I just assumed" — Abby paused, then added — "with everything that's going on out there, he had to pick tonight to take off?"

The nurse nodded. "He's been gone over an hour. I can't find him anywhere. His parents say he hasn't come home. Poor Kathy had to call them and give them the bad news. Listen, she might have seen Sid. Ask her. She's in the lounge, grabbing a cup of coffee. She's really upset about Billy."

Abby went directly to the lounge.

"I did see him," Kathy answered in response to Abby's inquiry about Sid. "He went outside to look for Billy. It's okay, though. The fire's out."

Abby stared at her. "*What?* He went out there by himself?"

"Well . . . sure. Just outside, though. He said Billy might be hiding by the entrance, afraid to come back in."

No one in Rehab thought of Kathy as another Einstein, but it seemed to Abby that she was being particularly dense now. "And did *he* come back in? Sid?"

Kathy looked blank. She brushed a lock of pale yellow hair aside, and thought for a minute. "Oh. Gee, I don't know. I mean, I haven't seen him. I had to make that horrible phone call to Billy's parents, and that rattled me, so I came in here to pull myself together." She thought again, studying the large, round clock high up on one wall as if it might provide an answer for her. "No," she said after a minute, "I don't think Sid came back in. I guess . . . I guess he's still out there."

Abby turned and ran from the room.

"C'mere," Susannah said to Will, her voice surprisingly firm. "To the lounge with me. Hurry up, before you have to go out on a run."

He followed her silently.

In the lounge, which to Susannah's relief was empty, the only sound was a burbling coffeepot. This was going to be hard. Abby was right. She *wasn't* used to talking about her feelings. Her family didn't believe in that kind of stuff. They talked about social events and what was on the agenda to buy next, and athletic events, but they never discussed how they *felt* about any of it.

Susannah had witnessed only one serious argument between her parents, the handsome, dynamic couple who gave the best parties and headed the invitation list of every other party. She had been seven or eight when she had overheard her mother almost shouting, "But we're never *home*! Why can't we just stay home with the children once in a while, and do nothing? Just . . . just *play* with them?"

Susannah had been shocked into a terrified silence by the sound. Her sleek, elegant, beautiful mother *shouting?* Not possible.

But she *heard* it.

And then she heard her father say in his usual, carefully modulated tone of voice, "Really, Caroline, this emotional outburst isn't the least bit becoming. It's very unattractive. Sometimes I worry about you. We have social obligations; you know that. Our parents had them, and now we have them. That's the way it is. Now, please, go upstairs, gather yourself together, and change for the banquet."

The outraged "oooh!" that had come from her mother then had sounded to Susannah like the cry of a wounded animal.

That was the only real argument she'd ever heard between them. Her mother was much quieter now, and the two went out almost every night.

But two years ago, when Susannah was visiting a friend who'd had an emergency appendectomy at Grant Memorial, she had seen her mother coming from the Psych building. And now she saw her arrive every Wednesday, disappear inside, and sometimes she saw her coming out. She was in there less than an hour. Susannah knew that, because she'd timed one of the visits.

Not long enough for volunteer work. Possibly just long enough for a session with a psychiatrist.

Susannah had never asked about the visits. Her mother was a very private person.

But maybe that was where Caroline Grant vented *her* feelings.

And now it's my turn, Susannah thought resolutely. She was quaking inside, this was so hard. She forced herself to look directly at Will, who was wearing a puzzled frown. "I want you to know two things," she said, willing her voice to remain steady. "First, I have never been as glad to see anyone jump from the back of an ambulance as I was a little while ago, when you did it. Because we didn't know who the paramedic was who'd been hurt. It could have been you. I'm really glad that it wasn't."

His frown eased and a hint of a smile appeared on his lips.

This wasn't so hard, after all. "Second," Susannah added, her voice stronger, "I wanted to give you a hug because I was so glad you were okay, and I couldn't, so I want to give you one now!"

His crooked smile grew until it reached his eyes. She had seen those eyes dark with anger, more than once. Will wasn't the most patient person in the world. Now, though, they were a warm, smoky brown as he looked at her with affection and amusement. "Are you making a pass at me, Susannah?"

That caught her off guard. She hadn't really thought of it that way. A "pass" sounded like something casual, something light, something people tried just to see if it would work. And sometimes there wasn't any more behind it than the challenge itself. That wasn't what this was. She wasn't interested in playing games with Will Jackson. He should know that.

She shook her head. "No . . . it's not like that. I would just like you to hold me, that's all." But that *wasn't* all, and she knew it, and she decided from the look that came over his face then that he knew it, too.

She waited then for him to back off. To say to himself, *Oh, no, this girl has something heavy-duty on her mind. I'm not ready for this. Talking about setting up a clinic together in Eastridge when we've finished medical school is one thing. She'll be a good doctor, and we'll work well together. But this girl standing in front of me with her hands at her sides, she looks too serious. I've got no time for this. I'm outa here.*

If he thought that, he didn't say it. Instead, he moved in two swift steps of his long legs to her and, without a word, reached out and folded her into his arms.

For the second time that day, Susannah felt like crying. And it wasn't because someone had almost died. She wasn't sure what it was. Maybe it was that it felt so good to be in Will's arms. Or maybe it was that she wasn't kidding herself. Things hadn't changed so much that no one would blink an eye if they walked in and saw her standing there, so clearly happy to be where she was. Maybe no one on the staff would care. They all liked and respected Will. But if her father ever found out . . . maybe that was why she had to blink back tears. Why couldn't life be simpler than it was?

Will reached down then and lifted her face to his. "You know what you're doing?" he asked.

"Yes," she said clearly. "I know exactly what I'm doing. Does that scare you?"

He threw his head back and laughed. When he looked down at her, still smiling, and not loosening his arms around her in the slightest, he said, "Lots of things scare me, Susannah, but you're not one of them. Could be I'm just being stupid here, but I'm not afraid of this at all."

She liked that he had admitted things scared him. But what she liked even more was that he wasn't afraid of her. Of *them*. Maybe they did have a chance. Will's long kiss said he felt they did.

Then, just as their lips parted, Susannah and Will heard Callie Matthews's voice, encased in an icy disapproval. "Well, well, *well*, what have we here?"

* * *

Deep in the woods, almost to the riverbank, Sid's wheelchair got hung up on a root jutting up out of the ground. Swearing softly, he reached down and used his enormous upper-body strength to tilt the chair slightly sideways, just enough to release it.

Billy hadn't stopped shouting, not for a second. "Sid, Sid, me up tall, get down!" Over and over, a terrified chant that grated on Sid's nerves like chalk on a blackboard. He was moving as quickly as he could, his mind trying to concentrate on some plan of action. What was he going to do when he found the tree hiding Billy? Even if he *could* climb it, and he probably could. In therapy, he'd climbed the rope all the way to the top, using just his arms. But sliding back down a rope, steadying his way down with his hands, was a lot different from sliding back down a tree trunk hoisting a panicked eight-year-old. Not to mention the fact that he couldn't see a damn thing out here in these smoke-filled woods. It was like trying to look through wool. If Billy hadn't been shouting, he'd never have been found.

Sid's eyes were tearing uncontrollably by the time he reached the riverbank and located the tree that sheltered the frightened boy. It leaned over so far, it was precariously close to the water, its top branches bending toward the opposite shore. When Sid peered across through the curtain of gray, he thought he saw a sudden flash of scarlet on the other side of the river. But Kathy had said the fire was out. What he was seeing must be embers.

He turned the chair sideways on the path to look up into the tree. "Billy? Billy, it's Sid. Can you climb down by yourself?"

"Nonononono! Too tall. You me down."

That was clear enough. Sid sank back in his chair. No way was he going to talk this kid down out of the tree. He thought about his options. He could go back to Rehab for more help and a ladder, but it had taken him so long to make his way down the path, and he was tired now, his chest aching from the constant smoke. It would take him a lot longer to go back. Billy would become totally hysterical, might even lose his grip and fall.

I know I can get up that tree, Sid told himself, trying to see up the slanted trunk. It's practically lying on its side. But how do I get back down?

"Sid?" Panic in the voice. "You me down, quick, quick! Fire come here! Quick, quick!"

And then all decision-making was taken from Sid. Because when he turned his head to see how far out over the river the top branches bent, he saw a wall of scarlet on the opposite bank. The flames were so vivid, he could see them clearly, in spite of the cloud of gray smoke. He watched in disbelief . . . Kathy had said the fire was *out* . . . as the flames raced up a dozen tree trunks at the same time, swallowing up the dry, parched leaves of the branches that bent out over the water.

When they had finished with those trees, they reached greedily for the branches stretching out across the water from Sid's side.

Including the branches of Billy's "up tall" tree.

They couldn't quite reach it yet. But they would.

"Quick, quick!" the frightened boy screamed. "Sid, hot, hot!"

Sid threw himself out of his chair, clutched the tree trunk around its middle, and began hauling himself upward with his arms as fast as he could.

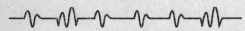

Susannah didn't pull away from Will. "What we have *here*," she told Callie, "is a *hug*. *You* know, Callie. A *hug*. It's what people do when they like each other. Friends, family, all kinds of people. They hug."

Smiling, Will added, "You should try it sometime."

This reminder that Callie Matthews didn't have a long list of people willing to hug her annoyed Callie. Her mouth twisted. A dozen nasty rejoinders flew into her mind, but she resisted every single one of them. Will and Susannah worked at the hospital. She might need them if she was going to keep Amber appeased. "Do you have a cappuccino machine?" she asked abruptly.

Will laughed. "A cappuccino machine?"

"Amber wants cappuccino." Annoyed that Amber had sent *her* downstairs instead of Jeremy, Callie added, "I don't suppose you have one."

"Oh, we do," Susannah said, deadpan, "but we sent it out for repairs. The cappuccino tasted too much like ordinary coffee. Can't have that." Her head was still resting against Will's chest.

Before a disgruntled Callie could answer, Sam stuck his head in the doorway and said, "Party in the cafeteria. The head nurse okayed it. We're celebrating the demise of the fire."

Callie brightened. "A party? I wonder if Amber could come. She's feeling a lot better." Callie supposed Jeremy would have to come, too. Amber would probably insist upon it. Well, it would be fun, anyway.

Forgetting the cappuccino matter, Callie ran off to invite Amber.

"The fire's out?" Will frowned at Sam. "You sure?"

"I'm sure. I got it straight from the horse's mouth — from one of the firemen."

Will looked doubtful. "When we were coming in on that last run, I thought I saw something on the other side of the river. A kind of reddish glow. It was hard to tell through all that smoke, but it looked like fire to me."

"Nope," Sam said emphatically. "It's out, and we're celebrating. Tell Kate, okay? Where is she, anyway? I didn't see her when I came in."

"She's upstairs with one of the firemen. Someone she knows. And" — Susannah smiled — "apparently likes a lot. Too bad he can't come to the party. Kate might not come without him. If it weren't for so many emergencies, I don't think she'd have left his bedside. But I'll tell her." To Will, she added, "It's that friend of yours. Damon?"

Will laughed. "You're kidding! Damon? He's had his eye on Kate for years. But after he dropped out of school, she wrote him off. Well, it's nice to know he'll be okay. No serious damage?"

"No. Some burns, but no lung involvement. I don't think he's up to dancing just yet, though." She promised Sam she would tell Kate and anyone else who didn't know about the party.

Sam decided that going all the way back to Linden Hill to take his shower would mean missing half the festivities. Astrid Thompson had only allowed an hour for the celebration. He left instead for the doctors' locker room. He'd take his shower there and borrow clothes from someone on the staff.

When he'd gone, Susannah glanced up at Will. "You know Callie is going to tell everyone in the hospital, and probably everyone in town, what she saw just now."

"So? Like we said, people hug." He hesitated, then said, "But before you go off to celebrate . . ." He bent his head and kissed her again, a long, slow, heartfelt kiss that shook Susannah to her toes.

"Like I said," Will said, smiling down at her, "people kiss."

Susannah laughed shakily.

He took her hand. "Now, let's get to that party before your brother hogs all the fun."

"A party?" Amber cried with delight. "In a hospital? What fun!" Then she sobered quickly. "What if my doctor won't let me go?"

"We won't ask." Callie went to the closet. "What do you want to wear? You can't go in that johnny." She took out a dress. "How about this red?"

But Amber had already turned to Jeremy. "Do *you* think I should go? I mean, I wouldn't want to do anything to make myself worse." She shuddered, and reached for Jeremy's hand. "As much as I like you, I need to keep my stay here as short as possible. You're a doctor, tell me what to do. Should I go to the party or not?"

Callie had been waiting impatiently for Amber's verdict on the red dress. She had also been waiting for Amber to say, "Callie, come and visit me in New York and I'll show you how to get into show business." Now, Amber was talking about hurrying away from Emsee as quickly as possible. And she was holding Jeremy's hand and looking at him adoringly. It was too much. Callie lost it. "Oh, get real, Amber," she burst out, "he's not a doctor! He goes to the same private school I do. And his name isn't even Noone. It's Barlow."

Jeremy's face turned scarlet.

Amber dropped his hand as if it had scalded her. *"What?"*

"I'm . . . I'm sorry," Jeremy stammered. "It's just . . . well, you looked so disappointed when I told you I wasn't a doctor, and I wanted to meet you, so I . . . I lied. But," he added hastily, "my father *is* a doctor here. He's Chief of Cardiology. That's how I knew so much about becoming one. I'm sorry, Amber. I hope you don't hate me."

Amber thought fast. Okay, so he wasn't a doctor. But his father was chief of something? That meant money, didn't it? Position? Even if this kid decided to sweep streets for a living, wouldn't his daddy be there to subsidize him? "I thought you said you were going to live in a mansion," she said sullenly.

"He already does," Callie interjected. "It's not as big as Linden Hall, but it's close." She wasn't regretting her outburst, nor did she feel the least bit sorry for Jeremy. It was his own fault. But if Amber wasn't going to be her new best friend, and it was pretty obvious that she *wasn't*, Callie at least wanted the actress to understand that she wasn't dealing with some small-town hicks here. She had already said that Jeremy went to school with her. Now she had to make sure Amber knew that it was a very expensive school and only the best people in Grant could afford it.

"Chief of Cardiology at Emsee is no small thing, Amber. And *my* father runs the entire complex." So there. Let her chew on that for a while. She probably wasn't half as rich as the two of them. How much money could soap opera actresses make, anyway?

Soap opera actresses only make money *when* they work, and the phone call to Leo was still fresh in Amber's mind, as was the image of her stepmother's tacky little house in Nag's Hollow. "Okay, Jeremy, I forgive you," she said softly. "I think it's kind of sweet that you cared that much about meeting me."

Jeremy heaved a sigh of relief and sank back down into the chair, taking Amber's extended hand in his.

Callie made a face of disgust. "So, do you want to wear the red or not?" she asked sharply.

"The red's okay. I think there are shoes that match in the bottom of the closet. Jeremy," Amber added sweetly, "you'll have to leave while I dress. Wait outside, okay?"

When he had left, promising not to go to the party without her, Amber asked Callie casually, "So, does a Chief Cardiologist make a lot of money?"

"A party?" Damon echoed Amber's words when Kate told him about the celebration. "Hey, man, I've been waiting my whole life to party with you. Help me out of this bed, okay?"

Kate was sitting in a chair beside Damon's bed. She'd thought for a while there that she wasn't going to have a free moment to run up and check on him. The very second that things had quieted down in ER, she'd asked her mother for permission to take a break. Astrid had glanced at her knowingly and asked, "You need a cup of coffee, do you?" Kate had laughed. "That's what I need, Mom, a cup of coffee." And her mother had said dryly, "Well, tell the cup of coffee I hope he feels better soon."

"You're not going to any party," Kate said now. But she was thinking that Damon looked tons better since he'd had his face and hair washed and had rested for a while. The burned leg was wrapped in gauze, and the patches on his cheeks simply looked like sunburn. "You're lucky to be alive."

"Then I should celebrate," he said, undaunted. He sat up. "Come on, Kate, what's the difference if I'm lyin' up here in this stupid bed, or sitting in a wheelchair in the cafeteria?"

"Your IV is the difference. You can't leave it behind, not yet."

"So, I'll take it with me. I've seen people walking through the halls dragging their IV poles behind them. Why can't I do that?"

Good question. There really wasn't any reason why he couldn't. He didn't have a fever and he wasn't dehydrated. According to his chart, which she had peeked at when she came into the room, his pulse and respiration were normal. He wasn't coughing, and as long as he didn't try to get up and dance his doctor probably wouldn't object.

"You're *not* dancing, though," she said, standing up. "Not on *that* leg. And I have to check with your doctor first."

"You can talk her into it." Damon grinned up at her. "I'd buy a used car from you any day. And anything else you were selling. Aren't you going to kiss me good-bye before you leave?"

"No. You already *had* a kiss. You won't catch me off guard again.

"Oh, yeah, I will. Count on it."

Trying not to smile, Kate went to seek permission for Damon to attend the party.

It wasn't that difficult. The tree was so slanted, it was like crawling across a log.

Sid made it up the tree. The bark was rougher than the rope in Rehab, and tore at his jeans and shirt, but he kept going. Billy continued his incessant cries for help until Sid, halfway up the tree, lost his temper and shouted, "Billy, shut up! I'm coming. Just quit that bellowing, okay?"

Silence from above. That was one thing about Billy. He knew when people meant business.

As he crawled, hand over hand, the lower half of his body dragging, his eyes watering, his chest aching, Sid waited for the sound of sirens telling him someone was on the way to fight the fire on the opposite shore. But all he heard was his own heavy breathing and the telltale sound of dry, crisp leaves falling prey to the flames. How close *were* those flames to the branch where Billy lay?

It seemed hours before Sid reached the boy. Billy was lying on his stomach, facing out over the river, clinging tenaciously to the branch that held him. It sagged further under Sid's added weight as he, like Billy, lay on his stomach across the tree limb, facing the young boy's sneakered feet.

Sid could see, now, the solid wall of scarlet flames on the opposite bank, long greedy fingers stretching out in search of more fuel. When those fingers touched the branches extending from this side, and Sid knew they *would*, he and Billy would be crispy critters in seconds.

"You'll have to climb down over me," Sid ordered. "Just back out and scoot over me. Then you can hang on to my ankles until your feet touch a sturdy limb, okay? Do it *now*, Billy! Start backing over me."

"Not!" the terrified boy cried. "Not! Go down bump."

"No, you won't fall. I won't let you. You'll find a thick branch and climb down, just the way you climbed up. Come on, Billy. The hot is coming. We don't have much time. Hurry!"

"Not, not!"

"Do it now!"

Slowly, cautiously, and Sid knew the boy was shaking even before his trembling feet bumped against Sid's head, Billy began backing up, a painful inch at a time.

The searching fingers of fire lunged across the small gap between the overhanging branches on both shores, and couldn't quite reach. Yet. But Sid knew the flames wouldn't give up. They'd try again.

There wasn't much time.

"Hurry, Billy, hurry, go faster!"

The boy felt the heat, too, and suddenly began scrambling backward like a monkey, over Sid, down his back and legs, hesitating while his feet searched for a sturdy branch, finding it, and dropping off Sid with a cry of triumph.

Now, Sid thought grimly, how do *I* turn around?

He tried desperately to feel *something* in his legs, some sensation that he could use to tell him when a branch was beneath his feet. But there was nothing. Nothing at all.

The sharp crackle of dry leaves told him the flames had finally reached a tree on his side of the riverbank. He hoped it wasn't *this* tree.

Don't panic, he told himself, panic will kill you faster than the smoke.

He had to turn around and crawl back face

first, using his arms. It was the only way. Easier said than done, considering his precarious perch and the fact that his useless lower body, like a sack of oatmeal, would be dragging behind him and throwing him off balance. But he had no choice. "Billy, you okay?"

"Not so up tall," came the answer. The voice sounded far enough below Sid that he knew the boy was making progress. But then, Billy had legs, didn't he?

Oh, don't go there, Sid told himself. This was no time to let bitterness get in the way. He began the task of trying to turn himself around, without the use of his lower body, on a tree that was probably going to burst into flames at any second.

Abby stood in front of Rehab, dismayed by the thick sheets of smoke that made it impossible for her to see into the woods. If the fire was really out, why was there so much smoke?

Sid couldn't possibly be out there. He wouldn't be able to see his nose in front of his face, never mind find a lost child.

Two tan-uniformed security officers emerged from the building.

"You have to help me," Abby told them anxiously. "I think two people might be out there in those woods. And one of them is in a wheelchair. You have to help me find them."

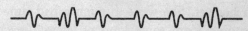

Susannah glanced around the crowded cafeteria. "I guess Abby didn't feel like celebrating," she said to Will and Sam. "I called the burn unit to tell her about the party, but the nurse I spoke to said Abby wasn't there. She promised to pass on the message when Abby got back. I don't see her anywhere, so I guess she didn't want to come. I need to know how her dad is."

"Can you blame her?" Sam's hair was still wet from his shower, but every last trace of smoke and grime was gone from his face. His borrowed blue sweater and jeans fit him well. "I mean, with her father . . . wow, who's *that*?"

Susannah turned to follow Sam's eyes to the wide doorway. Amber Taylor, resplendent in red silk, her dark curls piled on top of her head, sat in a wheelchair in the doorway, flanked by Jeremy and Callie. Callie's expression was sour.

"Oh, that's our resident actress. Amber Taylor. Isn't she pretty?"

"*She's* got a health problem? Nothing serious, I hope. She looks incredibly healthy to me." Sam had put down his cup and was standing at attention.

"Sam, you're leering." And the hunt begins, Susannah thought. Sam sees a pretty girl and thinks, Trophy. "They don't know what's wrong with her yet. She went through a bad time this afternoon, from some kind of allergic reaction. But she seems fine now. Anyway, it looks to me like Jeremy has already staked a claim, Sam."

Sam laughed. "Jeremy? With *that* girl? Yeah, right." And he was off, striding toward the door with expectation on his handsome face.

"Poor Barlow," Will said sympathetically. "He doesn't stand a chance against your brother."

Callie saw Sam approaching and recognized the look in his eyes. She was still stinging over Amber's acceptance of Jeremy, even after she'd found out he wasn't a doctor. Since when did Jeremy arouse such loyalty in important people? Callie bent and whispered in the actress's ear, "See that guy headed this way? His father is the richest, most important man in town." She noted with satisfaction the interest that sprang to life in Amber's eyes, and shot Jeremy a smug look as she stood upright.

Susannah was mildly curious about Amber's reaction to Sam. The girl definitely looked interested. When they had watched Jeremy make a grudging introduction, Susannah said, "That girl meets all of Sam's requirements. She's *very* pretty

. . . and she'll be leaving the hospital soon. No possibility of commitment there, which is basically what Sam is looking for in a girl."

What they couldn't tell from where they stood against the wall was, two minutes after Amber met Sam, she dismissed him. She'd had guys hanging around her since she was thirteen, first in Tennessee, then in New York. She had seen Sam's type before, many times. The handsome face, the easy, lopsided grin, the look that said I'd like to get to know you . . . but not for long, were all too familiar. He might be a nice guy, but she'd bet her career that his date book was as thick as a Manhattan telephone directory. Unlike Jeremy's. And Jeremy seemed willing to become her slave. If Leo was going to replace her on the show, she'd need someone faithful and steady, not someone like Sam Grant.

Her cool response to Sam bewildered him, annoyed Callie, and delighted Jeremy.

The four of them joined Susannah and Will at a spot near the refreshment table, which was really nothing more than a gurney covered with a white sheet. On it sat a coffee urn, a stack of Styrofoam cups, a plate of cookies, and a bowl of punch hastily tossed together from cans of fruit juice and soda. Music poured forth from a portable CD player someone had borrowed from the lounge, and people had begun to dance. Amber, who was feeling fine, saw no reason why she shouldn't dance. She didn't *feel* sick. She invited Jeremy to be her partner. While they danced, Sam watched, pretending that he was looking elsewhere.

Susannah almost felt sorry for him. He looked so puzzled. But it would probably do him good. It was certainly going to do *Jeremy* some good, winning out over Sam Grant. No wonder Jeremy looked like his feet weren't even on the ground.

When they returned to the table, Callie said, "Amber, how about if you sing? I saw the show when Lynette ran away from home and sang in that sleazy nightclub. You were great. This party could use some entertainment." Callie hadn't been asked to dance even once, and she was bored.

Amber looked pleased. "You saw that show? I told the director we should have picked more popular selections, but he insisted on those gloomy old ballads. You liked them?"

"I thought you sounded really professional. Sing for us, please!"

The thought of an audience appealed to Amber. When they were taping the show, the only audience was the crew, and they never appreciated anything. Okay, so it wasn't acting, the thing she did best. But an audience was an audience. Applause was applause. "I don't have any music."

"We'll use a CD. I'll find an instrumental to

use as background music, a song you know the words to. All you'll have to do is sing along. C'mon, help me pick out something."

They found a love song Amber knew by heart. Callie banged on the table to get everyone's attention, and made the announcement. "Ladies and germs" (she thought that was pretty clever, since they were in a hospital), "we have a treat for you tonight. The well-known actress, Amber Taylor, is a guest of this establishment, and she has agreed to honor us with a song. Please give her your full attention." Then she pushed Amber's chair into the center of the room, and ran back to turn on the CD player.

Although it annoyed Amber that there was no spotlight, and the cafeteria wasn't as crowded as she'd have liked, she opened her mouth and sang, completely aware of how lovely she must look in the red silk dress. The song was one of her favorites, and she knew she was singing it well.

It was one of Susannah's favorites, too, and she held Will's hand in hers while she hummed along under her breath. Amber's voice was sweet and true, and rang out clearly in the room.

When the last note died, Amber got her anticipated applause. People smiled, heads nodded, all eyes were on Amber. Which was exactly the way she liked things to be. *Needed* things to be.

She knew an enthusiastic audience when she

saw and heard one. These people liked her. A lot. The only audience she'd sung to before had been a group of bored extras hired to provide atmosphere in the "sleazy nightclub" on the show. They'd only applauded because they'd been paid to.

Well, well, well, she thought, smiling out at her audience as they continued to clap, maybe my career isn't over even if Leo *does* replace me. I don't *have* to act. It's not that much fun, anyway. All those lines of dialogue to learn every single night so I can't even go out to the clubs with my friends, and Leo yelling at me all the time that I'm not getting it right. Singing would be much easier. All I have to do is open my mouth and keep time to the music. And I must be good, or these people wouldn't be clapping so long and so loud.

What had she been so worried about? If Leo replaced her, she'd become a singer. They made lots of money, and probably didn't have to work half as hard as actresses. Maybe she'd become one even if Leo *didn't* replace her. She'd talk to Bess and Jules about it tonight, see what they thought. Not that it was their decision to make. It was hers. Still, they'd been in the business a long time, so it wouldn't hurt to sound them out.

She wouldn't need Jeremy, after all. Silly her, selling herself short like that, thinking that without the part of Lynette Martin, she wouldn't be worth anything. How stupid. What had got into her? Maybe it was this stupid sickness. She hadn't been thinking clearly. She didn't need a guy to prop her up.

Since Jeremy wasn't capable of reading Amber's thoughts, he was thoroughly confused by Amber's cool dismissal of him when she returned to the table. At first, he thought she must have decided she liked Sam better, after all. But she didn't seem any more interested in Sam than she did in him. She turned her back on both of them to insist that Callie go through the CDs again and find another instrumental. Maybe she'd sing another song later, she said, adding that she needed the practice.

Jeremy had no idea what she was talking about. What did she need to practice for? She wasn't a singer. All he knew for certain was, her attitude toward him had clearly changed. When they were dancing, she had smiled up at him the whole time, and pressed close to him. Now, she was acting as if he didn't exist. If it wasn't because of Sam, and he was sure it wasn't, *what was it*?

He guessed it must be *him*. What else could it be?

Amber asked Callie to wheel her to the rest room, and Susannah went along.

Watching them leave, his face crestfallen,

Jeremy breathed, "Women!" and Sam nodded. "Right."

While the party to celebrate the defeat of the fire continued, Sid struggled, deep inside the woods, to claw his way back to solid ground. The smoke all around him was fresh now, its pungent odor filling his nostrils and watering his eyes. His hair felt hot. But he kept going, hand over hand, down the slanted tree trunk as fast as he could.

It didn't seem nearly fast enough.

chapter
21

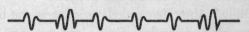

The security guards wouldn't let Abby go into the woods with them. She was forced to wait on the steps, pacing back and forth, the wind slapping against her, while they went in search of Sid.

He wasn't with them when they returned. They were walking very quickly, almost running. One of them was carrying a disheveled, distraught eight-year-old, his face streaked with tears and smoke grime.

"Billy!" Abby cried. "Are you okay? Where's Sid? Did he find you? Where *is* he?"

Billy began crying harder.

"We found him on the path," one of the guards said. "Can't make out what he's saying." To his partner, he urged, "Go, go, *go!*" When the guard ran, the man holding Billy explained, "We got trouble. The fire's crossed the river. The woods are on fire . . . on *this* side."

Abby stared at him in horror. "Oh, no! I thought it was *out!*"

"Must have been an ember. The way the wind

is blowin', it's no surprise. I sent George inside to call for help. But," he said, glancing down at Billy, "if this one here hadn't taken off into the woods, we might not have known the fire had jumped the river until it was too late."

"Billy," Abby demanded, swiping at the boy's face with a crumpled tissue, "did you see Sid? Tell me!"

Billy nodded. "Sid up tall tree. Me down, no bump."

Abby tried to interpret. What was he talking about? Sid up a tree? Sid couldn't have climbed a tree. "Sid climbed up a tree and got you down? Billy, that's not possible. Is he still out there? Is Sid out there in the woods?"

Approaching sirens screamed in the distance.

Billy began crying harder. "Hot, hot," he sobbed. "Hot up tall. Sid me down. Sid burn, burn!"

Abby swallowed hard. Her eyes darted to the woods ahead of her. And she saw, now, the faint glow of red-orange, high above the river. "Oh, God," she whispered, "he's out there?"

"Nah," a voice she knew well said from behind her, "he's right here."

Abby whirled. Sid, an exhausted grin on his filthy face, his jeans and plaid shirt nearly shredded from his desperate trek on his stomach down the tree trunk, was sitting in front of her in his wheelchair. The chair's metal arms were black with soot, its rubber tires coated with leaves and dirt. Sid looked every bit as bad.

Abby had never seen anyone so dirty and ragged. But he looked perfectly wonderful to her.

Saying his name softly, she knelt and wrapped her arms around him, trying to be careful in case he had been burned.

Behind her, Billy stopped crying and declared, amazement in his voice, "Hey, Sid! Not up tall? Go down bump?"

Sid laughed hoarsely. "No, Billy, I didn't go bump. Well, not so bad, anyway." He buried his face in Abby's thick curls. "Man," he whispered so that only she heard, "am I glad to see you!"

The security guard set Billy on the ground and turned away, tactfully giving Abby and Sid a few moments of privacy.

After a long moment of hugging, Abby lifted her face, tears in her eyes. "Did you really climb a tree, or am I just not getting Billy's vocabulary straight?"

"It wasn't the climbing *up* that was hard." Sid stroked her hair gently. "Not that much different from the rope, in therapy. It was getting back down that was the real challenge. If the tree had been straight up and down, I'd be ground cover now. But it bends. A lot. Like the slant board in the gym. That's why Billy was able to climb up it. Made it easier for me to get down. But I gotta tell you," he added grimly, "that fire is traveling *fast*. It was right behind me, snapping at my heels." He smiled faintly. "Gave me a real incentive to crawl faster than I thought I could."

Abby reached out to gently pull Billy closer to the wheelchair. "You okay, kiddo? You *look* terrible."

"Abby heart Sid?" the little boy asked.

It sounded like a bumper sticker. But Abby and Sid knew what he meant. "Yes," she said emphatically, "Abby heart Sid."

The guard turned back to them. "We didn't see you on the path," he said to Sid.

"By the time I got to the ground, I was too beat to try negotiating anything as tricky as that path. Too many roots and bumps. I steered my chair along the river path instead. It was a lot hotter, but it was smoother and I could go faster. That path leads directly to Rehab's maintenance shed. It's paved there, a parking lot for the maintenance workers, so I zipped over that and came around here from the other side." He smiled at Abby. "Sorry if I scared you."

Their sirens dying, the fire trucks pulled to a halt at the curb. Because they couldn't drive into the woods, Sid directed them to the maintenance shed, saying they could enter the woods from there with their hoses. "There's a hydrant," he added. "I checked when I passed."

When they had gone, Abby stood up, frowning. "Will Rehab have to be evacuated? We're the closest building to the woods and the riverbank."

The security guard said, "Could be. Man, that'd be quite a task, wouldn't it? I'll take this little one here inside, and then I'll check with the fire captain. Let's hope evacuation isn't necessary. I think maybe our little hero here," he said, patting Billy's head, "might have saved us from that."

When he had gone, Abby sank to her knees beside Sid again. "We have to get you inside, too. Are you okay? You're not burned? You didn't break anything?"

"Who knows?" He held his scratched and bleeding hands up in front of him. "I think it's mostly some minor scratches. But let's face it, if one of my legs was broken, I wouldn't know it, would I? I wouldn't *feel* it." There was no bitterness in his voice.

Abby grinned. "Yeah, you'd know it. It would hang funny, like this." She stuck her left leg out at an awkward angle and made it dangle loosely, like a puppet's limb.

Sid laughed. "You're making fun of me? I just climbed up a tree and saved a life, risking my own neck, and this is all the sympathy I get?"

Abby's face crumpled. She laid her head in his lap. "If anything had happened to you," she said quietly, "I . . ."

"Shh!" He reached out and pulled her upright to face him. "Abby, I'm okay. In fact," he said, hugging her tight against his chest again, "I'm better than okay. I'm great! I'm dirty and smelly and these scratches sting like hell. But I got that kid down out of that tree, and then I got myself back down, too, so I feel great."

"You're absolutely right," Abby agreed, hugging him back, "you *do* feel great!"

In the cafeteria, Astrid's voice came over the PA system. "The party's over, folks. We've got fire again, and this time it's in our own neighborhood. There's a meeting to discuss possible evacuation. ER staff lounge, stat! Move it, people!"

In the rest room, Susannah listened carefully, her mouth open in dismay. Fire? Here, at Emsee? Evacuation would be difficult, especially Intensive Care cases. How would they handle the monitors, the IVs, the respirators?

Amber and Callie seemed to be taking forever in front of the mirror. They had freshened their makeup, dabbed on perfume, and were now so thoroughly preoccupied with rearranging their hair, Susannah wondered if they'd even heard Astrid's message.

Exasperated, she ran to the door and held it open. "Come on, you two, didn't you *hear* that? The party's over, so quit fussing. I've got to get back to ER. Callie, you take Amber back upstairs. Then come down here and see if you can help. If we have to evacuate, we'll need lots of volunteers."

"Don't be silly," Callie said, stuffing her brush back into her shoulder bag. "My father would never let Emsee burn. This place is more important to him than anything. And I do mean anything," she added harshly.

But she turned to push Amber's wheelchair out of the room. They had made it as far as the open door when Amber's face turned scarlet and she began gasping for breath.

chapter
22

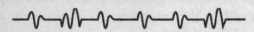

"**A**mber?" Callie cried, bending to look into Amber's distorted face. "Amber, what's wrong?"

"Oh, no." Susannah moved swiftly to kneel beside the wheelchair. "Another attack. Oh, God, Callie, run and get Astrid! Get help, hurry! Tell her anaphylaxis, so she'll bring oxygen and a doctor. *Go!*"

Callie turned and ran up the stairs.

Amber's eyes were wild with fear as she gasped for breath. Her fingers on the arms of the wheelchair were gripping so tightly, her knuckles were white.

Feeling totally helpless, Susannah loosened the neckline of Amber's red silk dress and began talking to her as quietly as she could manage, trying to soothe the terrified girl. There was nothing more she could do. Amber needed oxygen, and she needed it fast. She also needed, Susannah knew, a shot of epinephrine, which Susannah didn't have and couldn't have administered even if she *had* had it. Oh, God, she wasn't doing

Amber any good at all, couldn't, didn't know how. . . .

Kate and Damon emerged from the elevator. Kate had assumed that her friends would still be in the cafeteria. They hadn't expected to find Susannah in the hall outside the rest room, kneeling beside Amber Taylor, who was clearly in acute respiratory distress.

Kate hurried over to the two. "What's happening? Oh, God, she's having another attack, isn't she? I'll get someone. . . ."

"Already done," Susannah said tersely. "Callie went. Get me a wet cloth, though, okay? That might help."

Kate ran to the sink to obey. But before she could apply the wet paper towel, Amber's arms and legs went rigid, and her eyes rolled back in her head.

Susannah said, "I think we're losing her. *Where* is Astrid?" She noticed Damon, then, sitting in a wheelchair just outside the rest room door. "You're the fireman! *You* must know CPR. Help us here, okay? She can't breathe."

"But she *is* breathing," Damon said calmly. "Can't give her CPR until she stops."

"You're right. I forgot. But she's in agony! There must be something we can do."

"Get her out of that chair. Lay her on the floor so she'll be ready for the gurney when it gets here. That might make it easier for her to breathe, too."

With Kate's help, Susannah lifted the panicked girl. Amber's hands clawed the air. The painful sound of her futile gasps filled the air. They laid her on the floor. Susannah ripped off her pink smock and folded it, placing it under Amber's head.

Footsteps ran down the stairs, and Astrid and two other nurses arrived, Callie trailing behind them. "I've got the epi," Astrid said. "An orderly's on his way down in the elevator with oxygen and a gurney. How is she?"

Susannah had never been so glad to see anyone in her life. "Not good. We couldn't do anything for her."

Astrid knelt to administer the drug. "What was she eating?"

"Nothing. She and Callie were putting on makeup and . . ." Susannah paused. "And perfume . . . and this happened." She thought for a minute, then added, "Could she be allergic to her perfume? I saw her dab it on, and then, almost right away, she couldn't breathe."

The elevator doors opened and Joey Rudd rushed out, pushing a gurney. Dr. Izbecki was right behind him. "We've got a new fire going on up there," the doctor said irritably, "and it's too damn close to this complex!" When he saw Amber's face, he added, just as irritably, "Who gave this patient permission to come downstairs, anyway?"

"I've got to get out there," Damon said, sitting up very straight in his wheelchair. "I thought it was out."

"Never mind," Kate said firmly. "Forget it. You're a patient now, not a fireman. I'm taking you back upstairs the minute we're done here." She turned back to see if there was anything more she could do to help.

When Dr. Izbecki had taken over Amber's emergency care, Astrid stood up. "What did you say about perfume?" she asked Susannah. "I was too busy to listen."

Susannah explained. "I'll bet if we ask Jeremy, he'll say she put perfume on this afternoon, too. He *said* she hadn't been eating anything. It has to be the perfume."

Callie said, "Oh, that's ridiculous. I used it, too, she let me, and nothing happened to me."

"Maybe you're just not allergic to it," Susannah responded.

Astrid nodded thoughtfully. "I'll check. You could be right." She glanced at the barely conscious girl, who was being lifted onto the gurney. "Perfume? Well, why not? It's probably loaded with chemicals. This girl better switch brands, and *fast*."

With the oxygen mask on her face, and epinephrine in her veins, Amber's chest seemed to be rising and falling in a more normal rhythm. "If she has an attack like this away from immediate emergency care," Astrid added, "she might not survive it. I'll talk to Jeremy. If he confirms your suspicions about the perfume, I'll talk to the girl . . . and her managers. They should know, too, just in case she decides we have to be wrong about her favorite perfume poisoning her."

When Amber was stable, Joey took her upstairs, but this time to Intensive Care, where she would receive closer observation. Callie went along.

Astrid went, too. "I'll just make sure she's settled in," she told Susannah and Kate. "The meeting's still on, though. Five minutes. Be there."

Kate turned to tell Damon she was taking him upstairs before the meeting. She was afraid if he sat in on it and heard that the fire was bad, he'd insist on going back out there to help.

He wasn't there.

And though Kate's eyes swept the room from one corner to another, there was no sign of Damon Lawrence. The spot where his wheelchair had been parked was empty.

"I don't *believe* this!" she said softly. "That little sneak!"

Susannah had gone into the rest room to wash her hands. She came back out just in time to pick up on Kate's anger. Thinking that Kate meant Callie, since they had both used that particular noun in reference to Callie Matthews more than once, she asked, "What'd she do now?" And then, glancing around, added, "Where'd that fireman go?"

"To a *fire*, I think," Kate answered, her mouth a thin, straight line. She turned to face Susannah. "Has the fire really started up again? And it's headed this way?"

"I guess so. I thought your fireman friend was hurt. How could he go back out there? His doctor wouldn't discharge him, would he?"

"*She*. No, she wouldn't. But," Kate shrugged, "that wouldn't stop Damon." She waved a hand toward the spot where his wheelchair had been. "And I guess it *didn't*. He's gone."

"And you're worried about him, aren't you?" Susannah asked lightly.

"Yes." They started up the stairs. "No. I don't know. I shouldn't be. He doesn't deserve to be worried about."

"Will would go, too. If there was a fire threatening Emsee, he'd go even if he was hurt. And you don't think Will's stupid, Kate."

"That's different," Kate argued stubbornly. "Will *works* here. Emsee is his passion." She

217

smiled slyly at Susannah. "*One* of his passions."

Susannah laughed. "Don't change the subject. It's not different. Your friend is a *fireman.* Fighting fires is what he does. You can't blame him for going out there to help."

"I can if I want to."

"Oh, Kate. You're so . . . so *difficult.*" Susannah laughed again, taking the sting out of her words.

They both sobered quickly when they reached the top of the stairs and saw the activity in ER. Two firemen working in the woods had just been brought in. One had slipped from the riverbank into the water. Weighted down by his heavy protective clothing, he had come close to drowning. He had already been intubated with an endotracheal tube, and Astrid was on the phone ordering blood gases and a portable chest X ray. Two of the firemen's partners were standing anxiously in the doorway. One of them was dripping wet. "He must have jumped into the river and pulled the guy out," Kate said quietly, and went to get the rescuer an armload of dry towels.

The other victim had been felled by a burning branch. He had a concussion from the blow, and second-degree burns on his neck. Susannah and Joey Rudd wheeled him upstairs to X ray for a CAT scan. When that had been done, the fireman was taken to the Miller Burn Center for treatment.

Susannah took a quick break to call Abby. When Abby finally came to the phone, she was breathing hard. "It's bad over here, Susannah," she said quickly into the telephone. "We're going to evacuate. Going over to Psych. Can you come help? Bring as many people with you as you can. There shouldn't be any more injured coming into ER for a while, now that the fire's out in Eastridge. There aren't any houses along the riverbank, so there shouldn't be any more victims."

"We just had two firemen come in," Susannah pointed out. "There might be more."

"Astrid and the nurses can handle it. Just bring a bunch of volunteers with you, okay? And some orderlies. And we need gurneys and wheelchairs; bring those, too. Hurry, okay?"

Susannah hurried off to tell Astrid about the evacuation and ask if she could leave the ER.

Astrid already knew about the plan to move Rehab patients. "The patients," the head nurse explained, "will be taken to the Psych building. It's on the far edge of the complex, and out of the path of the fire. They'll be transported through the enclosed passageways. They're going to need more gurneys and wheelchairs over there, lots more. I want everyone we can spare to hike on over there. Take burn treatment kits with you, too, and basic first aid supplies, in case they run out. Stay there if you're needed, and you probably will be. Do whatever you can to help. If the word comes that the fire is out, they can stop the evacuation. But until then, this has to be done. Kate, I want you to stay here with me. And I'll need two nurses and two orderlies. The rest of you, get yourselves over to Rehab."

The news that the fire was encroaching upon the medical complex stirred everyone to action at once. Ten minutes later, a group that included Susannah, Will, Jeremy, Sam, two volunteers from the lab, and three orderlies hurried silently through the glass-enclosed passageway leading from Grant Memorial to other hospitals on the grounds. The curving glass roof above them, normally bright with sunshine or reflecting a starry sky, was so dark with smoke, the round lights set high up in the wall had come on automatically.

"I think," Jeremy commented nervously, "the fire is moving a lot faster than anyone expected."

No one answered, but everyone increased their pace.

They were almost to the end of the passageway, and could see the rear entrance to Rehab just ahead of them, when a sharp, crackling noise sounded directly overhead. Feet slowed and heads lifted . . . just in time to see a tall pine tree, totally engulfed in flames, toppling straight toward the glass roof of the corridor.

The tree landed. It hit the roof and crashed through, sending glass and flaming branches in every direction. In seconds, the narrow passageway was filled with smoke and flames.

chapter

23

Two things saved the lives of the people lying among the destruction wrought by the flaming tree. One was the partial breakage of the glass roof, which allowed in life-saving air. Thick though it was with smoke from the fire outside, it was still air.

The second thing that saved them was the fact that the tree had been so thoroughly consumed in flames when it fell, the fire burned itself out almost immediately. There was nothing left on the tree to burn.

But as the flames hissed and died out, the huge, thick-trunked tree collapsed into two sections of thoroughly charred wood. One piece fell to the right, effectively barring any retreat back to ER, while the other blackened chunk fell to the left, directly in front of the Rehab entrance.

When Susannah, coughing to clear her lungs of smoke, lifted her head, she grasped the picture instantly. The tree was no longer burning. They weren't going to be consumed by flames after all, as they all must have thought when they saw that inferno diving directly at them. Nor were they going to choke to death on smoke.

But they weren't leaving, either.

"Will?" she called hoarsely, peering around her. The glass walls were still intact. The corridor was dark with smoke, the tree sections taking up most of the available space. The wall lights, amazingly, were still on, their yellow glow faint through the smoke. The people who had entered the tunnel with her were beginning to raise themselves up cautiously and look around them. They all looked stunned. Two of the orderlies had deep cuts on their faces and were bleeding. Sam was just climbing to his feet, staggering slightly as he did so. Susannah saw a swelling just above his left eye and thought, concussion? Had he been hit by the falling tree?

She didn't see any sign of Will. She called his name again.

"He's over there," Sam said, pointing. His voice was as raspy as hers. "The tree hit him."

Susannah looked. Her heart turned over with dread. All she could see of Will was an arm in navy blue, poking out from beneath one of the charred tree's larger limbs. And she noticed then that he wasn't under there alone, because the white shoe sticking out on the other side wasn't Will's.

She scrambled to her feet. "Somebody find the first-aid kits!" she called, and ran to Will's side.

"We have to get this thing off him! There's somebody else under here, too. I think it's one of the orderlies." The stench of smoke was nauseating. Susannah fought against it. "Sam, can you get past that chunk of tree, into Rehab?"

"I don't think so." Sam kicked at the thick slab of thoroughly charred wood. Ashes fell to the floor, but the obstacle remained intact, lodged firmly in front of the door. "Might as well be a boulder," Sam grumbled, turning away. "I can't move that thing, and I can't climb over it." He raised his eyes to where the roof had been. "I'll have to climb out, and go for help."

"Climb out?" Susannah knelt to feel Will's pulse. It was strong and steady. Maybe he wasn't seriously injured, though that seemed impossible. "Climb out how?"

"I don't know!" Sam snapped. "Let me think. Maybe I'll make a hole in one of the walls. They're glass, right?" He began looking around for something to use as a hammer.

"You can't break that glass," one of the orderlies said as he stood up. "It's shatterproof. I know, because I slammed a softball into one of these walls accidentally, last summer, and the wall didn't even crack. Powerful ball, too. Home run."

"Oh, great," Sam declared, "why didn't they use the same glass on the ceiling?"

"They probably did. I didn't *say* I threw a giant tree at the wall."

People stood up, brushing themselves off, shaking their heads to clear them. "Who's missing?" Jeremy asked. His lower lip was bleeding, his left eye beginning to swell, from the impact with the tile floor. "Anyone missing?"

"Will's under here," Susannah answered shakily. She pushed and prodded at the burned branches, but couldn't budge them. "And I think Joey Rudd might be, too. Help me try to lift this off, okay?"

"It's burned to a crisp," one of the orderlies said, moving over to stand beside Susannah. "How heavy can it be? It'll probably fall apart in our hands." He was bleeding from a cut on his forehead and had to keep wiping the blood away with one hand.

The tree didn't fall apart in their hands. It didn't move. Blackened though the branches were, the trunk remained firmly in place on top of Will and the orderly.

"We *have* to move this thing!" Susannah shouted, fighting back tears. "Did anyone find a first-aid kit?"

Those who could were moving around now, poking among the charred branches, looking for the scattered contents of the medical kits. One of the lab volunteers, a deep gash on his left arm, handed Susannah a packet of gauze and a plastic bottle of disinfectant. She knew, judging from his laceration, that she should use them immediately on his arm. But until she knew that Will and Joey could breathe under that tree, she didn't dare take the time to tend to anything else.

Sam was standing alone under the shattered ceiling, staring upward.

Seeing him there and realizing what he was doing, Susannah cried, "Sam, get over here and help us get this tree off these guys! Quit trying to figure out how to be a hero."

"Oh, you don't care about getting out of here?" he asked sarcastically as he moved toward the tree pinning the two down. "You're willing to set up camp here? Aren't you forgetting there's a fire out there?"

"Someone will come and get us out. There must be firemen all over the place out there. It's more important to get Will and Joey out from under this thing."

Giving in, Sam took over then, telling everyone but Susannah and the lab volunteer, a young man whose face was very white, to grab hold and yank, hard, on the count of three.

It worked. They were able to lift the tree, though only a few inches. They could not, however, move it. There was no place to put it in the narrow passageway. All they could do was hold it up while Susannah and the injured orderly swiftly but gently tugged Will and Joey free, sliding them along the tile until they were a safe distance away. Then the tree was dropped back into place, still barring the way back to ER.

"I need more first-aid things," Susannah said urgently, kneeling beside Will. There was a deep cut above his ear, and another on his chin. He was breathing, but his eyes were closed. "There must be a kit here somewhere. I need more than gauze and disinfectant." Joey didn't move at all, and though she saw no visible injuries, when she checked his pulse, it was weak and thready. Chest injury, Susannah thought to herself. "Sam, have you found a way out yet?"

"Oh, *now* you want me to be a hero. No, I haven't. I'm still thinking. Jeez, you'd think they'd have an emergency ladder or steps in here or something."

"They probably weren't thinking along the lines of a flaming tree crashing through the ceiling when they designed these passageways," the injured orderly said dryly. "I mean, it's not something that happens every day."

Jeremy brought Susannah a collection of medical supplies that he'd been quietly gathering for her. She thanked him and checked to see what he'd found. More gauze, more antiseptic, a bottle of sterile saline, cotton balls, burn salve. But no blood pressure kit, and no IV setups, which was probably what Joey really needed. She knew how to do the blood pressure thing, but not the IV. But maybe one of the orderlies knew how, or one of the lab volunteers. Will did, of course . . . but Will was unconscious.

"Oh, Will, why don't you wake up?" Susannah murmured as she checked his pulse again. "We need you."

In Rehab's noisy lobby, where nurses and therapists had gathered patients on gurneys and in wheelchairs and were awaiting word on the evacuation procedure, Abby, pacing back and forth impatiently, said to Sid, "Well, where *are* they? Astrid said she was sending help right away. And no one's come. That fire has to be getting closer every single second. If they don't come pretty soon, we won't get out of this building in time."

"Call over there," Sid suggested. "Find out what's going on."

Abby nodded, and ran to the telephone at the reception desk. When she reached Astrid in ER, she burst out, "Where's the help you promised us? We're ready to leave, but we need more people!" She listened for a minute, then, a look of alarm on her face, asked, "Are you sure? They're not here. *No* one's here." She listened again, then added, "Which way were they coming? Through the passageways? I'll run and look."

She hung up, spoke to Sid quickly, and then turned and ran to the stairs.

At the foot of the stairs, a fireman stopped her. "Where you headed, miss?" Two other firemen were standing in front of the heavy glass doors leading to the enclosed corridor. Their backs were to Abby, as if they were studying the passageway.

"In there," she answered, pointing. "I'm looking for some friends. They were on their way here to help us with the evacuation."

He shook his head. "Can't go in there, miss. Tree landed on the roof. It was burning when it fell. You didn't hear the crash? What's left of it is blocking the door. People in there."

Abby gasped. "My friends? Are they hurt? Is there a fire in there?"

"No fire. Can't tell if anyone's hurt yet. We'll get 'em out, don't worry. Think we might have to go back outside, though, and approach this from the top. Lower a ladder, maybe."

"If someone's hurt," Abby said worriedly, "they won't be able to climb a ladder."

"Yeah, you got a point. Well, don't worry. Like I said, we'll get 'em out. Got the fire out, didn't we?"

Abby looked blank. *"Did* you? The fire's out?"

"Oh, yeah. It's out this time, for sure."

"Why didn't someone tell us? We're all ready to evacuate up there. No one knows it's out."

The fireman shrugged. "Sorry. We were on our way to spread the word when we heard the crash, saw what happened. Maybe you could just tell everyone, while we see about getting these people out of there?"

"Is Susannah in there? Susannah Grant?" Realizing immediately that the fireman couldn't know who was in the passageway, Abby turned and ran back upstairs.

"The good news," she said breathlessly to Sid, "is, the fire's out. Really out this time. We don't have to evacuate, after all. You tell everyone, while I call Astrid again. I need to ask her who she sent over here. Because the bad news is, a tree fell on one of the passageways and the people who were coming to help us are still in there." Abby's expression was bleak. "I think Susannah, maybe Kate and Will, too, are with them."

chapter
24

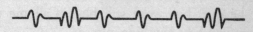

Astrid had already heard both pieces of news: that the fire was finally out, and that some of her people were in jeopardy. "Izbecki and Lincoln are on their way," she told Abby. "I don't know how they're going to get in to see what the damage is, but we've been assured the fireman will do all they can to find a way."

"Who's in that passageway?" Abby asked, needing to know. "Who did you send?"

"Susannah and Will. Sam insisted on going along, too. I saw no reason not to let him, although he's not a volunteer. He's strong, and healthy, and can push a wheelchair or a gurney. Then, let's see, Jeremy, two volunteers from the lab, and three orderlies. We really don't know very much about what happened, and have no idea what the injuries might be. All we know is, there's no fire, which is good."

Susannah *was* in there. Suddenly exhausted, Abby leaned against the wall. It had been a long, terrible day, and night. Wasn't it ever going to end? "Kate didn't come with them?"

"No. We had two emergencies here just as they were leaving. I needed her here. Look, be sure to keep us posted. I can't leave here. We've still got firemen coming in with smoke inhalation, and we've had a couple of others. The fire may be out, but we're still busy. Call me the minute you hear anything, please."

Abby promised, and hung up.

The Rehab residents, relieved to hear they would be spared the discomfort and inconvenience of evacuation, had been returned to their rooms. The lobby was empty, the smell of smoke still heavy in the air. Sid was waiting for Abby when she got off the phone. "You want to go see what's going on," he said. It wasn't a question.

She nodded mutely, and moved behind his chair to push it outside and around to the back of the building.

On the fourth floor at Grant Memorial, a nurse bustled briskly into Amber Taylor's room. "I guess you heard," she said brightly, "the fire is out. Finally. What a relief! It was getting too close for comfort, if you ask me." She handed Amber a small white pill. "So, it was just your perfume, hmm? Well, I've heard of stranger things. All you have to do is switch perfume, and you'll be fit as a fiddle. Too bad about your friend."

She added this last so abruptly, it took Amber

a few seconds to let it register. "My friend?" She didn't have any friends here, did she? That Callie person certainly didn't count. Who would want *her* for a friend? "What friend?"

"Why, Jeremy, of course. I know he was in here visiting you." The nurse shook her head. "It's awful, isn't it? They must be so scared. I would be. I'm claustrophobic."

The pill still in her hand, Amber sat up. "What *about* Jeremy?" Just because she wasn't going to need Jeremy, didn't mean that she didn't care what happened to him. He'd been nice to her. She wasn't as heartless as some people she worked with thought she was. "What's happened to him?"

"Oh, you didn't know?" The nurse explained in graphic detail. "I mean, can you imagine? They're lucky that tree didn't keep burning. They'd all have suffocated, with the flames eating up the oxygen in that corridor."

Amber swallowed the pill and took a drink of water. "If there's no fire in there, they're not really in any danger, are they? I mean, the firemen will get them out, right?"

The nurse shrugged. "Well, sure, but the thing is, we don't know who's hurt or how bad the injuries might be. I heard it was a really *big* tree. Chances are, it landed on at least some of them, don't you think?"

An image of Jeremy flattened under a burning

tree was so repulsive to Amber, she shuddered violently.

The minute the nurse left, Amber got up and dressed in jeans, a sweater, and sneakers, clothes she usually wore only in the privacy of her apartment. She tied her hair up in a careless ponytail and left the building by the backstairs. She had no idea where Rehab was, but she remembered seeing a map of the complex in the ER lobby. If she could sneak a peek at it without being recognized, she'd know where to go to see what was happening to Jeremy.

She wasn't sure *why* she was going to Rehab. It wasn't the kind of thing she would normally do. What if a reporter or photographer saw her out in public, dressed like this? She was taking an awful chance.

But she needed to see if Jeremy was okay.

In the lobby downstairs, the skeleton staff was busy tending patients in treatment rooms, and the coast was clear. Amber found Rehab on the map without difficulty, and seconds later, was on her way there.

Although the lone fireman standing outside the glass windows of the passageway kept signaling to those inside that someone would be coming to get them soon, Susannah was really frightened that they wouldn't arrive in time. Joey's breathing was becoming more erratic with every passing moment, and she didn't know what to do for him.

"I feel so helpless," she told Sam. "I'm afraid he's going to stop breathing. I think his chest was crushed by that tree."

Sam had given up on the idea of finding a way out. Climbing smooth glass walls was an impossible task, even for an athlete as fit as he was.

"It's not your fault," he told Susannah. "You've done a lot already." He had watched in admiration as she patiently, efficiently, used antiseptic and gauze to disinfect an endless number of cuts, talking calmly to each person she tended, even though Sam knew she was frantic about Will and Joey. Especially Will. "I always thought you just carried piles of sheets around at Emsee, maybe delivered flowers to patients. No one told me you played nurse."

And you wouldn't have listened even if I had, Susannah thought. Like the rest of the family, you're never interested when I talked about Emsee. Aloud, she said, "I'm not *playing* anything, Sam; this is *real* blood here," pointing to the deep laceration on the orderly's arm. She had applied antiseptic and covered the wound with gauze, but it needed stitches. The gauze was already blood-soaked. She had told him to keep pressure on the wound, and he was obeying.

"I was trying to pay you a compliment," Sam said stiffly.

"I'm sorry. Don't pay any attention to me. I just want to get out of here."

"Don't we all?" Sam turned away and went to the window. Everyone else, silent and anxious, was sitting on the floor, waiting. Only Jeremy had roused himself enough to help Susannah by holding the bottle of antiseptic when she was using it. "Where the hell is that ladder?"

Will stirred, just then, and his eyes opened.

Susannah, sitting beside him, saw the movement and leaned forward eagerly, saying his name softly.

"What happened?" he asked groggily, reaching out with one hand.

Susannah took the hand gratefully in hers, and leaned closer to him. "You won't believe this," she said, forcing a weak smile, "but a tree fell on you. How do you feel?"

"Like a tree fell on me." He moved his head slightly to one side. "Where are we, anyway?"

She told him, then asked him where he hurt.

"Beats me. My head, I guess." He moved his arms and legs, gingerly at first, then more actively. "Nothing broken. Anyone else hurt?"

Susannah glanced sideways at the other figure lying on the white tile. "Joey. Joey Rudd. The tree fell on him, too. I think his chest was crushed. I don't know what to do for him, and the tree blocked both exits." She gestured toward the windows, where a crowd was rapidly gathering. "Izbecki and Lincoln are out there. Waiting for a ladder. Two ladders, actually. One to climb up the side, and one to lower down in here. I wish you had your paramedic equipment with you. Joey's really in a bad way."

And at that precise second, as if he'd heard her, Joey Rudd stopped breathing.

chapter
25

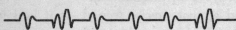

Even before Susannah recognized the sudden silence as the cessation of Joey's breath, she felt it in her bones. "Something's wrong," she said to Will, and he sat up, reeling dizzily.

Susannah crawled over to Joey. "He's not breathing!" she cried. "Oh, God, Will, he's not breathing at all! We have to do something!"

"The ladders are here," Sam said from the window. "Can you keep him alive for a few more minutes?"

Will, appearing very shaky, arrived at Susannah's side. She had already tipped Joey's head backward, opened his mouth, and checked to make sure there was nothing obstructing his airway. "I'm not sure I'm up to CPR, but I'll give it a shot," Will said. "There's nothing else we can do. I have no equipment. No epi on me, either. It's CPR or nothing." Raising his voice, he called quickly, "Anyone else here willing to take a shot?"

No one was. The orderlies and the lab volunteers weren't accustomed to dealing with life-

and-death matters, and were clearly frightened by the idea. "You go ahead, Will," Jeremy urged. "You're the expert here."

As Will bent to administer mouth-to-mouth, Susannah noticed with alarm a half-dollar-sized spot of clotted blood on the back of his skull. "Are you sure you're okay?" she whispered as he began breathing into Joey's mouth. Not pausing, he nodded. "I'll do the chest compressions," she said. "Just tell me when." She remained kneeling beside Joey and waited for the signal from Will before applying pressure, counting as she pressed. "One, two, three, four . . . five . . ."

"They've got the ladder up against the wall," Sam called. "Fireman's climbing up. Got another ladder alongside. I don't know how they're going to get that second one down inside here. Too heavy."

Susannah didn't even want to think about the problems involved in getting Joey up a ladder. All she wanted now was for the orderly to begin breathing again.

Will signaled again for chest compressions. While Susannah took over, he called to Sam, "Shout up to the firemen through the hole in the ceiling. Tell them we need a doctor down here. We need a defibrillator, and epinephrine, stat. Make sure they know you mean it!"

Sam began shouting, repeating Will's request. "He said okay," he reported a moment later.

"And here comes the second ladder. Hey, that's cool, they're using a motorized winch to lower it down. Everybody out of the way, unless you want to get creamed again."

Susannah and Will continued, to no avail, their CPR efforts until the equipment arrived. She could see that Will was exhausted, and teetering slightly. "Can't someone else take over for him?" she pleaded. "Until the doctor gets here?" But the group gathered around them, watching, shook their heads, unwilling to take on the awesome responsibility of attempting to breathe new life into so limp a form as Joey's.

"I can't . . . do this . . . much longer . . ." Will gasped, "and I'm getting worried about brain damage. It's been too long . . . he needs oxygen, damn it!" He called over his shoulder, "That ladder in place yet?"

"Another minute and we'll be all set," Sam answered. "Here comes your doctor, up the ladder on the outside. Looks like he's carrying all kinds of medical stuff." Then he added, almost as an afterthought, "Hey, there's that gorgeous girl who sang, the actress?"

Susannah cried, "Sam, for pete's sake, we're trying to keep someone alive here!" But Jeremy's head came up and he turned toward the window. At first, he didn't recognize Amber. She wasn't wearing nearly as much makeup, her hair was simply done, and she was dressed in the kind of clothing worn by all the other, more ordinary, girls he knew. But then she smiled and waved, and he knew it was her.

For just a moment, Jeremy told himself she had come to see if he was all right. Then he rememberd how cool she'd been at the party, and told himself he didn't care why she was there. He turned back to more important things, like the saving of a life.

The ladder finally in place, Dr. Izbecki climbed down with some equipment, followed by more lowered down on a rope. "How is he?" he asked brusquely when he arrived to kneel between Will and Susannah.

"No response. His skin is warm, dry, and cyanotic. Pupils dilated, unresponsive. He's been out more than four minutes," Susannah said.

Before Dr. Izbecki implemented the defibrillator machine, he inserted a breathing tube for Joey. Then he applied the electrical charge Susannah had been waiting for. She prayed for a response. Nothing.

Following rapid-fire instructions from the doctor, Will established an IV line, administering epinephrine. Dr. Izbecki called for defibrillation with "full output discharge."

Susannah thought of the order as bringing out the full artillery, giving it everything they had. If it didn't work, nothing would.

Will had already put gel on the paddles. They

waited for the defibrillator to charge. When it had, the electrical current meant to send Joey's heart into a regular rhythm was delivered. His body lurched, and a slow, ventricular rhythm, which Susannah thought of as better than nothing, showed on the monitor.

"Pulse is weak, but palpable," Will announced when he checked. "Thirty."

Susannah sank back on her heels. Joey Rudd was among the living again. Just barely, but . . .

"We need to get him to surgery," Dr. Izbecki said tersely. "Let's get him up that ladder, stat."

Two firemen had climbed down to help them remove the patient. Will went with them, ascending first in order to support Joey's IV line.

When they reached the top, they still had the downward trek to make on the outside. Susannah and the others watched carefully through the glass windows as Joey was gently, as quickly as possible, carried down the outside ladder. When he had been placed on a waiting gurney and rushed away, they all breathed a sigh of relief.

Once outside, Will handed over the IV line to another paramedic and waited at the foot of the ladder for Susannah. She fell into his arms in the smoky darkness, asking him again if he was sure he was all right.

"I am now," he said, holding her close.

To Jeremy's amazement, Amber was waiting there, too. For him. "Don't get any ideas," she said quickly when he had stepped off the ladder. "But you were nice to me, and I wanted to make sure you were all right. Just don't let it get around that I have a heart, okay? People in the business might decide to take advantage of me."

Jeremy smiled wearily. There was a slight edge to his voice as he said, "Okay, so you're tough as nails. I'll buy that." He had already figured out that she'd only latched on to him because she thought he was a doctor. She had pretended not to care that he wasn't when she found out, but after the way she'd acted at the party, he was sure now that she'd just been waiting for the right moment to dump him. He didn't feel like forgiving that. But he had to admit she was a good actress.

Amber glanced at him sharply, but said only, "Come on, let's get out of here before someone sees me. If a picture of me looking like this showed up in the paper, my career would be history. You'd better go to ER and get checked out. I'll walk you back there and sneak back up to my room. But come and see me before I leave tomorrow morning, okay? Come say goodbye?"

Jeremy didn't think so. "Thanks for coming to see how I was," was all he said.

ER was busy for the next forty-five minutes, caring for those who had been in the passageway. Susannah discovered she had more cuts than she'd thought, including one on her right knee that required four stitches. Will's cut was more serious, and it was decided to keep him overnight for observation. No one but Joey Rudd needed surgery.

Astrid came into Susannah's suture room after her knee had been sewn. "I understand you did us all proud in there," she said, smiling. "Everyone I talked to said you're going to make a fine doctor. No surprise there, of course."

"I didn't do much." Susannah slid off the table, wincing as the injured leg hit the floor. "It's funny how much we take our equipment here," she said, glancing around the room, "for granted. I don't even notice it half the time. But when you're in a situation like the one with Joey, and you find yourself without any medical supplies at all, you really appreciate things like a defibrillator and an IV setup. Is he going to be okay?"

Astrid nodded. "I think so. Thanks to you and Will. They took him upstairs, by the way. Four-oh-seven." She smiled again. "Just in case you're interested."

Susannah returned the smile. "I am definitely interested. And I think you should know," she added proudly as they left the room, "Will was pretty amazing in there, too."

"I know. I heard. No surprise there, either."

When they entered the main lobby, Abby and Sid were waiting for Susannah.

"How's your father?" Susannah asked at the exact same moment that Abby cried, "Oh, Sooz, are you okay?" Laughing, they tried again. Abby's father was doing "as well as could be expected," and Susannah assured her best friend that she was okay.

"It must have been awful in there," Abby said, her dark eyes wide. "They still haven't removed that tree. They're having an awful time with it."

"I think they should just leave it there and decorate it for the holidays," Sid suggested.

Abby laughed, but Susannah shuddered and said, "No! I don't want any reminders. Besides, we need that passageway, right? That tree has to go."

When she told them she wanted to go up and see Will, Abby persuaded her to meet them an hour later at their favorite restaurant. "It was closed because of the fire, but I just heard it's open again. And I'm starving. Bring Kate if you can find her. Her mother said she went over to Rehab, looking for someone, but I didn't see her there."

Abby and Sid left then, and Susannah hurried to the elevator and pressed the button. She was anxious to see how Will was. That was a nasty cut on his head, but Dr. Izbecki had said he'd be fine. She trusted Izbecki. Still, she needed to see for herself.

"Where are you going?" Kate's voice called from behind her.

Susannah turned. "Where have you been? Oh . . ."

Kate wasn't alone. She was with the tall, lanky fireman Susannah had seen her with earlier.

"You're supposed to be a patient here," Susannah said to him. "What are you doing up, dressed in your fire gear?"

"He was, of course," Kate said, "fighting the fire. Like I hadn't already guessed that. During a lull here . . . while *you* were being rescued . . . I went looking for him." She sent Damon a stern look. "I explained to him that we are very possessive of our patients here. We don't let them slip away easily. Not until *we* say they can go."

"So," Susannah asked, directing her question again to the fireman, "is the fire really out?"

He nodded his head. His face was dirty again, but even through the grime, Susannah could see that he really was very good-looking. *Nice-*looking, her mother would say. He looked like a nice guy. "Yep. We lost one refinery office building, six homes in Eastridge, a park, and a church, and a whole lot of trees."

Susannah felt sick. There'd been a lot of damage. One little spark, one little flame, and all of a sudden, an entire city was at risk. And all of Emsee.

"No deaths, though," Damon added. A faint, weary grin appeared on his face. "Thanks to you and Will, I hear. Joey Rudd's a nice guy. He's always treated me okay. I went to high school with him."

"Yeah, but *he* graduated," Kate said, but she was smiling when she said it. "Now, would you mind going back on upstairs to your room, where you're supposed to be? We have bed check at eleven, just like in boarding school. And prison."

"Never been to boarding school, never been to prison. But I don't think I should have to go up there alone. Don't prisoners have guards that take them everywhere?"

"Oh, spare me," Kate muttered. "All right, since Susannah has been kind enough to summon the elevator, I suppose I could guide you upstairs."

A smug, satisfied smile wreathed Damon's face.

The elevator arrived and they all stepped inside.

"Hey," Astrid called from her desk, "are you girls *both* deserting me at the same time? What if there's a huge emergency? What'll I do?" But she was smiling.

Kate grinned at her mother. "Dial nine-one-one."

Damon shook his head. "Man, you have one really smart mouth."

"Thank you very much," Kate said.

The elevator doors closed.

Inside the cage, the smell of smoke was beginning to dissipate.

Upstairs, in room 407, Will was sitting up in bed, knowing Susannah would be walking through the door any minute now.

He was smiling.

MED CENTER

A building blows up . . . and Med Center's volunteers feel the shock waves.

It's bad enough that Med Center is crowded with victims of a chemical explosion. But worse yet, many of the wounded are still trapped inside the building. Is it worth it for the Med Center volunteers to risk their lives in a dangerous rescue attempt?

BLAST

MED CENTER #4

BY DIANE HOH

Their lives are nonstop drama . . . inside the hospital and out.

Coming soon to a bookstore near you.

MC396